"Royals love everyone.
them Royal. And now that h
for him to go una tove others."
Angus studied his mother, then asked, "Is that what love
means? Doing things for others?"

In this remarkable and poignant flight of fantasy, master story-teller Blaine M. Yorgason uses the round, round eyes and giant heart of a Royal albatross named Angus Austin to reveal life as it ought to be. As Gus's soaring flights carry him far and farther, high and higher, seeking always to comprehend the joys and difficulties of his life, our hearts will ascend with him in a triumphant search beyond the most distant horizons for our own understanding.

ASCENDING

A Novel

ASCENDING

A Novel

BLAINE M. YORGASON

Gentle Breeze™
PUBLICATIONS™

This book is a work of fiction. However, because
it is written allegorically, any resemblance of names,
characters, places and incidents to actual persons, organizations,
events or locales, is entirely intentional, and should be so considered.

Artwork and cover design by Douglass Cole, Cairo Design Group
Design and typesetting by Kelly Conway, Accu-Type Typographers
Editing and Proofreading by Jana Lillie

Library of Congress Catalog Card Number: 96-078784

ISBN 0-9649968-2-0

Printed in the United States of America

10 9 8 7 6 5 4 3 2 1

Acknowledgments

I express my deepest thanks to Stewart H. Beveridge and Craig E. Middleton, who have once again helped a dream of mine to become reality. I also express appreciation to Pam, Andrea, Kevin, Joseph, Allison, and Rick, who first heard this tale—and told me they liked it.

In loving memory of
my sweet little
Charity,
who is now ascending far and farther,
high and higher,
gaining perfect understanding
as she goes.

...He could'nt seem to shake ...the shell off his forehead...

1

ANGUS AUSTIN didn't understand. Every time his mother looked down at him, her round, round eyes filled with tears. But to Angus it wasn't an unhappy day, not at all. Why, besides being the very day of his hatching out, the sky was clear and blue, the sunshine was bright and glinted beautifully off his mother's mottled gray and brown feathers, and the sand in the bottom of the nest was warm and comfortable. In short, everything seemed perfect. Even the shell he had hatched out of had broken away easily, and with the exception of a small fragment on the side of his forehead that he couldn't seem to shake off, he was free of it. And that was why Angus didn't understand. If everything was so wonderful and good, why was his mother weeping?

"Screech?" he asked, trying without success to make himself understood. "Screeawwk?"

But it was hopeless. Though Angus clearly understood some of what his mother said, as well as a great deal of everything that was going on around him, he didn't yet know how to communicate his thoughts to her. So his tiny squeakings fell on apparently deaf ears.

"Oh, my darling Angus Austin," his mother declared as she again blinked away tears, "if only I knew what to do. I know your belly is empty, for that is the way of those who have just hatched out of their shells. But alas, my belly is as empty as yours, my darling, and so I have nothing with which to satisfy your hunger."

2   And that was a problem for the young mother. With no food in her famished stomach, how could she possibly disgorge the proper sustenance for her chick? And if he didn't eat, her mind whirled, how long could he possibly survive?

On the other hand, if she left him to gather food, would he survive the wind, the sun and the cold, as well as the predatory birds who were always searching for an easy, defenseless meal? The chances were nearly one hundred percent that he would not, and the young mother could not bear that thought, either.

"Screech," Angus said to her as best he could. "Screeawwk."

Tenderly the mother albatrix looked at her little chick, knowing he was trying to tell her not to worry. And she was trying not to, she truly was. Why, hadn't she just this day gone through the elaborate process of giving him an appropriate name? And this despite her terrible hunger?

For weeks she had been pondering names for her unhatched chick. But then, as her hunger had grown and her need for a Chosen One had grown apace, she had begun thinking of Royal names, names such as Angus Austin, Geoffrey Rossiter and Alexander Campbell, hoping perhaps that would help her Chosen One to come. Of course she had known her chick would not be hatched a Royal, because she was only a Sooty. And there was also the fact, she thought with sadness, that her rookery was nowhere near the islands off the southern tips of New Zealand and South America where true Royals were almost always hatched out. Yet she truly liked the aristocratic names used by the Royals, and so today she had carefully given one of them, her favorite, to her chick.

3

Now, if she could only find a way to feed him.

A deep, throaty whistle offshore suddenly caught her attention, and the mother bird watched with ill-concealed envy as billowing clouds of hungry Sooty albatri, petrels, shearwaters and gulls lifted off in answer to the call of the incoming fishing trawler. How long, she wondered as she listened to the distant throbbing of the trawler's engine, had it been since she had eaten? Twenty—no, it was twenty-one— twenty-one days since she had consumed anything at all. Not that her own hunger troubled her, for though it was painful, it didn't. In fact, she would have sacrificed more than eating to keep her egg warm, the egg that held everything dear she had left in the world. But now her little chick had hatched out, and . . .

From around the rocky point to the south of her another whistle sounded, faint and far away, almost inaudible in the din from the wheeling flock. But the young mother heard it and shuddered, for with that whistle, weeks before, had come the terrible news that her mate would no longer be beside her. Even now she did not understand what had happened, nothing more than that many birds had died in the bay near the floating cannery. But the whispered word, passed along by the wheeling, gliding members of her colony, reached her with the sound of the distant whistle, and put fear as well as loneliness into her heart.

4   Blinking back tears of grief that still came on occasion to her round, round eyes, Angus's mother turned away from the rocky point, felt suddenly faint, and nearly fell with all her weight upon her little chick. Yet by grabbing the side of the nest with her bill she managed to retain her balance, and so the little one didn't even realize how close he had come to being crushed.

"Oh, gr . . . great Creator," the young mother sobbed hopelessly, "I am so terribly, terribly weak. Th . . . that is why I seek a Chosen One, not for myself but for my chick. He is so little and so helpless. I fear what will happen if I leave him to try and hunt for food."

Suddenly aware that a large shadow had briefly dimmed the sun, Angus's mother lifted her head and spun it almost all the way around. "Angus Austin," she whispered then, fearing almost to believe, "do you see that beautiful bird over there on the rock?"

And little Angus, who was still uncertain on his awkward, wobbly legs, and who was nowhere near tall enough to see over the edge of the nest anyway, squeaked and squawked that he did not.

"But you must see him, Angus! You must! He is a Royal—a rare and lovely bird who stands head and shoulders above every other bird in the world."

"Squeeeak," Angus replied quite innocently. "Squeeeaawwwk."

"I know you are tired, little one," the mother albatrix said tenderly, knowing her little hatchling had worn himself out trying in vain to see over the top of the nest. "But before you sleep, please notice the Royal, and tell me he is truly there."

5

For a moment she paused, her tears once again falling freely. "I . . . I believe he is our Chosen One, Angus Austin," she whispered. "At least I hope he is. I have pleaded with the Creator to send a Chosen One to help us, and I . . . I think it's the Royal you see."

But Angus was too tired to attempt another look. In fact he was too tired to even attempt another squeek or squeeaawk. And so while his down-covered head finally drooped in well-deserved sleep, his mother alone watched the Royal. Had the magnificent bird truly come to help, she wondered as hunger gnawed ever more fiercely at her belly? Was it possible that her son would now survive? Or that she would?

Oh, how she hoped so. And yet as minute after

agonizing minute dragged past with the huge bird making no attempt to approach, her eyesight grew bleary and her own head began dropping toward her breast.

So it was not their Chosen One, her exhausted mind told her. The Royal was not even there on the rock at all, but was merely some form of hallucination brought on by the greatness of her hunger.

"Ma'am, you do not look well."

Startled, the young mother blinked and looked around. Someone had spoken, someone had—

"I'm sorry to see that you are so hungry."

With stark realization the head of Angus' mother jerked erect, and for the first time she saw the look of compassion on the Royal's regal countenance. He *was* there, she thought, as tears of gratitude flowed from her eyes. The great Creator had heard her pleas, and had sent a Chosen One to preserve the life of her son.

"I have a gullet full of food," the brilliantly white Royal with startlingly black wingtips declared tenderly as he started across the pebbly beach toward her. "The finest squid delicacies from the far-off sea. Would you allow me to disgorge for you, and you in turn for the chick?"

"I . . . I—"

"It would please me very much to help you," the Royal said softly, and then with great kindness he smiled and pecked her on the bill.

"Thank you," the hungry mother whispered as the beautiful Royal stood over her. "It is so good of you to . . . to think of us!"

6

"I would rather think of no one else," the Royal replied softly, kindly, as befitted his Royal station. And then he opened his bill widely, and the lives of little Angus Austin and his mother were spared.

7

"Omasquawk!"
Angus breathed in awe
as he stared out across
the rocky beach...

2

"It's okay, Mom," Angus was saying as he pulled his eyes away from the small patch of blue sky above the nest. "If the Royal told you he had to leave, then he must have felt we could get by on our own."

Angus cherished the tender look his mother gave him, as well as the smile of pride that creased her bill. He was young, he knew, and yet he was fiercely determined to be brave, and to give his mother no reason to worry.

"Besides," he continued, "I'm growing real fast, Mom. Already I'm molting out of my second coat of down. First thing you know I'll be covered with real feathers. And I'm getting big, too. I'll be all right while you're gone, Mom. I promise."

For a moment Angus was silent, thinking. Around him the shrieks and cries of the Sooty albatross colony went unheeded. The soothing sound of waves lapping on the nearby shore, a sound he had come to love dearly, was unheard. Instead his mind was filled with the image of the huge Royal, who, while saying little, had come again and again with food for him and his mother, freeing her to comfort and warm him at all times. But now the magnificent bird was gone.

"Mom, will . . . will the Royal ever come back?"

"I'm sure he will," Angus's mother answered, the tremor in her voice belying the confidence of her words.

"I hope so, Mom, because I love him. I love him a whole lot!"

Abruptly Angus's mother had to fight tears. "I loved him too, Angus Austin. And he loved us."

"Do you really think so?"

"Of course! Royals love everyone. I . . . I think that is part of what makes them Royal. And now that he has shown his love for us, it is time for him to go and love others."

Angus studied his mother, then asked, "Is that what love means? Doing things for others?"

Startled that such a profound thought had come from her son, the young mother looked at him. "Why . . . yes, I believe so."

"Then maybe I didn't love the Royal," Angus declared solemnly. "I didn't do *anything* for him."

Smiling at her son's sweet and innocent honesty, Angus's mother drew him to her feathered breast.

9

"Of course you did, Angus Austin. You accepted his love and his assistance. And each time he brought you food, you let him know, through your joy, of your gratitude. You loved him, and because he was a Royal, he knew it."

For a moment a breeze sent playful fingers creeping down into the nest, stirring Angus's tufted down. The young albatross luxuriated in the feeling, turning by instinct to face the breeze, and only when it was past and the air had grown still again, did he speak.

"Mom, when I grow up, I'm going to be a Royal, just like him. After all, our Royal told me that my name, Angus Austin, is certainly a Royal name. So I already have a good start, haven't I?"

Again Angus's mother smiled. "Yes, you do, darling. Be like our Royal as much as you can, and both your father, may his soul rest in peace, and I will be happy."

"No, Mom. I'm going to be *just* like him. I'm going to be a Royal!"

"But . . . you were hatched a Sooty, Angus Austin—a dear, wonderful little Sooty."

"So?" Angus was adamant. "I'm still going to be a Royal, Mom. I'm going to help other birds, and I'm going to love everybody, just like the Royal did for us."

Again his mother drew him to her breast. "If you will do that," she declared tenderly, sympathetically, "then to me you will most certainly be like a Royal. Now, I really do need to be taking off."

"Why do you have to go so far away?" Angus then asked, changing the subject only slightly.

10

"I . . . I'm not sure," the young mother replied, her gaze distant and unseeing. "But always the Royal brought us the finest squid, Angus, squid he had gathered from far out at sea. Though he did not say why, he did say that such food was vitally important for you. Don't you think we should trust him?"

"Is that a way to show that I love him?"

"It is." Angus's mother sighed. "And being happy while I am away is a way of showing your love for me."

"Okay," Angus declared with a smile. "I'll be happy! Only, I'll miss you, Mom."

"And I'll miss you. But think of other things, Angus Austin, and the time will pass more quickly. Watch the sky above you changing its faces; listen to the sea changing its voices; and remember that with each change I will be closer to coming back to you. And Angus Austin, even if you get a little hungry, just wait for me. Okay?" And with another quick but loving peck on her son's bill, the young mother spread her wings, lifted off into the wind, and was gone.

For a long time Angus stared at the empty sky above the nest, trying to get used to the feeling of being alone. And while he was determined to do as well as he had assured his mother he could, part of him longed desperately to see her lovely form fill the sky and settle back onto the nest with him. Finally, however, he admitted to himself that she wasn't going to immediately return, and so he lowered himself onto the sand in the bottom of the nest. Adjusting his body to get comfortable, he preened a few tufts of

11

down from beneath his right wing. Then, closing his eyes, he concentrated on being happy.

Only, somehow it didn't happen. No matter how he tried to dredge up happy memories from his six weeks of life, which of course are almost the same as years in the lives of certain two-legged mammals, all he could think of were his mother and the Royal, and in his memories all they were doing was feeding him. And while those memories were definitely happy, they weren't very helpful. Instead, they just made him feel more lonely and miserable—and hungry.

Thus, Angus's wait for his mother seemed longer than his entire life. During the times of daylight the sun beat upon him mercilessly, for there was no shade above the nest where his mother had always stood to protect him. And during the times of darkness the wind sent chilly, probing fingers around the rocks and through the long grass of the island, relentlessly seeking him out in the open nest and escalating his misery. To make matters worse, the passing days intensified his hunger, so that soon the little nestling could think of little else. Where was his mother, he wondered constantly? And where were the delicious squid he had grown so accustomed to eating?

The one good thing about his lonely wait was that he grew to love the changing face of the small patch of sky that showed above his nest; that, and the changing voice of the sea that lapped and thundered and roared somewhere nearby. The endless varieties of cloud amazed Angus, as did the mists, the light rains, and even the thunderstorms that roared in upon him. The different sounds of the sea were the same. He was enthralled by all of it, and wondered that he felt such a call to be a part of it.

When the third day brought no sign of his mother, Angus suddenly realized that there might be more beautiful sky to watch than the small patch of blue that hung above his nest. More, he wondered if perhaps the sea might even be visible to him from up on the edge of his nest.

Rising to his feet he waddled to the steep side of the nest and attempted to climb, only to find himself tumbling end over pinfeathers back to the bottom. Shaking his downy head to clear it, Angus heaved himself to his feet and tried again. And again he met with the same unceremonious results. He was simply too uncoordinated to waddle up the side of the nest.

13

For a long time he surveyed the situation, wondering what he should do. At first he thought of giving up, but the idea that he might better see the sky and maybe even the sea, as well as the approach of his mother, kept nagging at him. So again he tried to climb out, and again and again, without ever quite making it.

But then, quite by accident, he hooked his bill into the turf that comprised the side of the nest, and suddenly he realized that he could use his bill to drag himself up to the top. Suiting thought to action he did so, and after a few moments of hard work had pulled himself onto the lip of his nest. Once there he opened his bill and let go of the turf, took a deep breath to catch his wind, straightened up to look around, and—

WOW!

His eyes wide with amazement, Angus Austin stared about him, first in one direction and then in another. And no matter which direction his gaze went, he was absolutely overwhelmed with the glorious things he could see.

For instance, all around him teemed the colony of Sooty albatri, a morass of movement that until then had been only sounds coming from beyond the rim of his world.

"Omasquawk!" Angus breathed in awe as he stared out across the rocky beach, at the moment literally covered with the teeming mass of his fellows. All around him mostly unseen nestlings were shrieking their hunger from the bottoms of their nests, and parents were taking turns dropping from the air into the nests and disgorging food into the nestlings' probing bills. Nearby a mother albatrix sat patiently on an egg that had not yet hatched; down the beach another bird rolled an unattended egg from a nest and then squatted into it herself; next to her two other albatri fought angrily for a bit of turf they both wanted for the following season's nesting; and on the beach a young male and female were engaged in an elaborate greeting ceremony, clacking their bills and cackling and screaming while they bowed repeatedly in a sort of dance with each other.

These were his fellows! These were the common Sooty albatri of which he was a part, the kindred from which he had hatched out. And Angus Austin, who had never seen so many of them at one time before, felt a surge of pride in his great heart that he was part of such a wondrous group.

Next there was the sea! Beyond the colony the rocks of the beach, no longer made white by the hundreds of generations of Sootys, drove darkly into the sea. And Angus, following the contour of the land with his round, round eyes, was astounded to see waves crashing against them. He had heard the sound of the waves' crashing before, of course, but the sight was so beautiful that it took his breath away, and for a long time he forgot to even think about how hungry he was.

There was more, too. Though the horizon behind his nest was close, no farther away than the dark basaltic rocks that rose to what he thought of as unimaginable heights, in the other direction, out across the sparkling sea that was the South Pacific Ocean, the horizon seemed far and forever distant. In fact, with the summer sun low in the December afternoon sky, there were times when Angus could not tell where the sky ended and the sea began.

And then there were the clouds! From the bottom of his nest Angus had seen clouds before. But never had he seen them spread across the face of the heavens in all their ethereal beauty. Highest above him were the cirrus clouds, wispy and windswept ice crystals that glowed golden-white in the afternoon sun. Lower toward the horizon were the puffy, flat-based cumulus clouds, bubbles of warm air that had risen and cooled until the water vapor within them had become visible. These were even more startlingly

15

golden, and deeper shades of red glowed in their blue shaded valleys.

And finally, low in the distance and looking threatening even to Angus, were two dark golden-red, anvil-topped cumulonimbus clouds. Though they were too distant for Angus to hear the thunder that rumbled forth from them, he could still see the occasional lightning flashes, and the virga sweeping along beneath them hid the edge of the sea until it seemed as though ocean and sky were one and the same—a huge mass of storm and fire.

Angus's eyes brimmed with tears, and he shivered with joy and awe as he gazed upon the glorious sight. He had never imagined such beauty existed, had never dreamed that the small patch of sky above his nest could hold such wonder.

16

Suddenly the burning round body of the sun dropped beneath the fiery clouds. It hung for a moment suspended in all its glory, and then dropping slowly it slid into the glistening, light-studded sea. But even when the sun was no longer visible, brilliant shafts of light streamed upward from it through the constantly changing clouds, seeming to Angus almost as if they were mighty feathered wingtips pointing upward and outward, beckoning him to come and behold the wondrous vistas hidden in the distant sky.

"Omasquawk, Mom," he gasped once she had finally returned and he had filled himself from her gullet. "I saw the sky, and the sea! *All* of it!"

"You did?"

"Yes! It was so beautiful it made me cry! I climbed to the edge of the nest, and it felt like I could see the whole world!"

Angus's mother smiled. "I'm happy that you learned how to do that, sweetheart. But please be careful."

"Okay, Mom," Angus smiled. "I will."

"Good. Now tell me, how did you feel when you saw the sky, and the sea?"

And little Angus, the joy of discovery lighting his eyes, began to describe the clouds, the sun, and the feather-like wingtips of light that seemed to beckon him to come.

"Why is that, Mom? What is it that's making me want to go?"

Angus's mother smiled a little sadly. "Perhaps it is the voice of the Creator, my son."

17

"The Creator? Who is that?"

"He is the great Being who created us, Angus Austin; us and all other living creatures."

"Really?"

"Uh-huh. He loves us, too, and will always respond to us when we ask sincerely for his help and direction. When I knew that your father was not coming back I asked for help. And because I asked, the Creator sent the Royal, our Chosen One, to help us in our hour of need."

"I wish the Royal had stayed with us, Mom. I really miss him!"

"So do I, Angus Austin." The young mother looked away so Angus wouldn't see her tears.

"What does the Creator want of me, Mom? Why is He calling me?"

"I don't know, my son. You must discover that for yourself."

Angus grimaced. "How can I do that, when I can barely pull myself to the top of the nest? I don't even have any feathers to fly with!"

"You will," the wise young mother replied with a smile. "And when you have them, then you must obtain directions from the Creator, after which you will fly far and farther, high and higher, ever seeking beyond the most distant horizon, until at last you have found your understanding."

"Understanding? What's that?"

"The secret of who you are and why you are here, Angus Austin, the secret only you can discover."

18

A few days later Angus was alone again, perched on the rim of his nest, watching with fascination the wheeling and soaring of the mature Sooty albatri of the colony. And it was a particularly fine day for soaring, too, for huge cumulonimbus thunderheads filled the sky and strong winds whipped across the rocky island. Facing into the winds the mottled brown Sootys climbed without effort until they wheeled to get the wind at their backs. Then they dived with amazing speed until they slammed into the water. For a few moments there followed a furious splashing and heaving about, after which the Sootys lifted into the wind again, the whole lovely process being repeated.

Angus was watching this, and watching especially the birds nearest his nest, when he noticed the parents of a nestling named Howard Theodaceous. Howard, who was called Howie T, had occasionally squawked greetings at him from across the way. Howie's parents were climbing and wheeling and diving, but instead of doing so for the pure joy of flight, Angus suddenly realized that they were letting the wind lift them into a position where they could hurtle downward into the midst of the flotsam and jetsam collected in a lazy whirlpool a few hundred yards offshore.

Wondering at this, Angus quickly became aware that it wasn't just his neighbor's parents who were doing this. In fact, as he watched more closely he realized that diving into the flotsam and jetsam was the object of every bird in the sky. The only reason some of the birds didn't do it at the end of their dive was because they somehow overshot the wind-collected refuse and had to try it again.

19

At first Angus wondered why the adults were playing such a strange and pointless game. But when Howie's father lumbered back to the nest after a perfect dive and began feeding Howie from what he had collected, Angus suddenly knew. That wasn't refuse the birds were diving into at all, nor was it a game they were playing. Instead they were gathering food from a new source which his dear mother had somehow overlooked, and which he needed to tell her about!

"Mom," Angus screeched excitedly after she had returned and filled his empty belly on the sixth day of her third absence. "You don't have to go so far away to gather our dinner, you know."

"Why, of course I do," his mother replied absently. "I look nearby, Angus Austin. But somehow I never seem to find that special squid we eat."

"That's what I mean!" Angus beamed. "We don't have to eat squid! We can eat flotsam and jetsam just like everybody else. I'd be real happy with that."

Angus's mother looked closely at her son, suddenly worried. "Do you know what flotsam and jetsam is, Angus?"

"Yeah! Food!"

"Angus Austin, it isn't food for us, or at least it shouldn't be! Flotsam and jetsam is nothing more than refuse—garbage! It is wind and wave collected, and is made up of everything dead and rotten that is cast into the sea, including the awful offal from slaughtered fish. Eating it can do nothing but pollute you."

"Yuk!" Angus grimaced. "It sounds offal—I mean, awful!"

"It does, because it is. I believe that's why the Royal told us that you should only eat squid."

Angus's face clouded over. "I . . . I forgot about that," he almost whispered.

"I thought you had." Carefully Angus's mother squatted beside her son in the nest. She knew what she wanted to tell him, but she had no real idea how to go about it. For a long time she remained deep in thought, and little Angus, growing impatient, fid-geted restlessly beside her. Finally, with a deep sigh, she leaned down and began preening her son.

"Do . . . do you still love the Royal?"

"Sure I do!" Angus arched his back, luxuriating in his mother's preening. "But I don't understand why he didn't at least say good-by to us."

"Neither do I," the young mother agreed softly. "But since when does real love demand instant understanding?"

Angus smiled crookedly. "You're right, Mom. And we really do love our Royal, don't we?"

"Yes, we do." His mother got a faraway look in her eyes. "Yes, we do. Now, can I have a promise from you that you won't ever pollute yourself with that horrible garbage?"

"I'll promise if you will."

"Then I promise."

"And so do I," Angus declared proudly, and very, very innocently. "I promise that I will never eat the awful garbage of this world, not for as long as I live!" And he smiled to see the pride and joy in his mother's round, round eyes.

21

...Angus ended up plowing a small furrow in the sand with his bill...

3

"Hey, Angus Austin," Howie T called from his nearby nest one hot December morning, "you alone today?"

"Yeah," Angus answered with a little discouragement. "Mom's gone again, for who knows how long, too." Angus *was* a little discouraged, for not only was he lonely without his mother, but he was frustrated because precious days were vanishing one after another and life seemed to be passing him by. He never did anything, he never went anywhere, he hardly ever even spoke to anyone. Instead he slept a lot, ate when he could, and spent the rest of his time sitting on the edge of his nest, enjoying the sea and the sky and watching the rest of the world hurry past.

"Wanna go someplace?"

Surprised at the invitation, and with sudden excitement stirring his blood, Angus hardly dared to respond. "I . . . I don't know. Where're you going?"

With a gleam in his eyes, Howie T looked at his friend. "To the shoreline," he replied smugly.

"To the shoreline?" Angus questioned in amazement. "I . . . I don't know, Howie T. I haven't even been out of my nest. I . . . I don't think my mom wants me to leave without her."

Howie T laughed derisively. "Yeah, I noticed you're sort of a mama's boy."

"I am not! Uh . . . what you gonna do there?"

"Oh, the usual." Howie T grinned. "Waddle a little, meet some chicks, maybe pick up a little something to eat out in the flotsam and jetsam. You know—fun stuff! You coming?"

23

"Ugh! Not if you're going to eat flotsam and jetsam! That's garbage!"

"Oh, yeah?" Howie T was instantly defensive. "Says who?"

"My mom, and the Royal who was our Chosen One."

"Yeah? Well, my mom tells me to eat it. And so does my dad. Besides, my mom says there isn't any such thing as a Chosen One. So there!"

"Well, there is, because I know him. And one day I'm going to be a Royal just like him. Maybe I'll even be a Chosen One, too."

"Yeah, sure! You're a Sooty, you dumb cluck, and Sootys can't ever be Royals! Everybody knows that."

"Well, I have a Royal name—"

"Yeah, and it's a stupid one, too! *Angus Austin?*" Howie T's voice actually sneered the name, which made it sound terrible. "Who ever heard of a dumb name like that? From now on I'm calling you Gus, and if you want my advice, that's the name you'll tell the guys your mom gave you."

Surprised at his neighbor's reaction as well as his claims and advice, Angus didn't know what else to say. So he said nothing, but from that moment he began to wonder if somehow he wasn't quite as good or as important as the other nestlings.

"Oh, come on," Howie T snorted disgustedly, not even recognizing Angus's ponderings. "Live a little, Gus! Your mom won't be back for a couple of days, so you have plenty of time. Besides, it's a big world out there, and you can't always hide from it. Now, come on! Let's go have some fun!"

Smiling with a sudden burst of excitement, Angus lifted his stumpy wings for balance and hopped from the rim of his nest. But where Howie T balanced easily as he landed and then waddled forward, Angus stumbled immediately, fought for his balance and lost it, and ended up plowing a small furrow in the sand with his bill.

"Ouch," he moaned as he struggled to get his feet back under him.

"I'll say," Howie T agreed as he watched in amazement. "You just learning to waddle or something?"

"I . . . I told you I haven't ever left the nest before."

"It shows!" Howie T groaned, and it was obvious

24

to Angus that the nestling was embarrassed by him. "Well," Howie T finally said with a sigh of resignation, "come on, and I'll introduce you to a few of the other birds."

He started out, and Angus followed behind as best he could. But because his legs were set so far back, and because his feet were so big and his stumpy wingtips did not yet reach the ground to give his big body support and balance, his waddle continued as more a series of forward-falling spills interlaced with pathetic efforts to stand upright, punctuated regularly with furrows plowed in the turf by his increasingly sore bill.

"What's the matter with you?" Howie T asked just before they finally emerged from the rocks. "You hatched funny or something? Look at you, Gus. You're a real mess! You can't walk good, you've got hardly any feathers, your feet are too big, all your weight's in the wrong places, and my squawk but you're big! Are you sure you're an albatross?"

Angus, feeling sore and dizzy from his latest tumble, merely blinked his eyes and nodded.

"Then something's definitely wrong. I never noticed how big you are, I'll tell you that. And those downy pinfeathers? Ugh! I don't know anybody who isn't into at least his third molt, and some of us are already working on our fourth. You know, maybe meeting the other nestlings isn't such a good idea. Why don't we go back, and . . . uh . . . try this another day."

But Howie T was forever too late, for at that moment a group of Sooty nestlings waddled around a point of rocks and came face to face with him and Angus.

"Holy eggshell," one of them gasped as he looked up at Angus. "What you got here, Howie T? The Aussie Blimp?"

There was a chorus of laughter, and Howie T, forcing a smile to hide his own embarrassment, lifted a wing. "Hi, Lyncher X. Hi, guys. This is my neighbor, Angus Austin. I call him Gus, for short."

"Not very, he isn't!" one of the gang shouted, and the whole crowd burst into more laughter.

"And what kind of a stupid name is Angus Austin?" another one questioned, bringing more peals of laughter from the group. "If I had a name like Angus, I think I'd crawl under a rock or something!"

"Yeah," another one screeched, "it makes *me* think of the south end of a northbound seal!"

"Or a dumb sea cow!" another one howled.

And again everybody squawked with laughter, Howie T along with them. Only when he had finally stopped—when all the birds were holding their sides and gasping for breath—did Howie T begin to remember his manners, which are very important to all albatri. "Gus," he mumbled with a touch of embarrassment, "these are the birds I waddle around with. This is Lyncher Xenophobe—Lyncher X for short. This is Andre Lewis—A L, we call him; this is Sebastian Clunk, or Seb C; and this skinny bird is Eleazor Dimfoddle, which he must be—dim, I mean—because he doesn't like his name shortened."

"H . . . hello," Angus ventured while the birds squawked with further glee.

"What's your other name again?" Lyncher X demanded, abruptly ending the laughter. "The name besides the dumb one?"

"Austin," Angus declared hesitantly. "My . . . uh . . . my mother called me Angus Austin because it is such a royal name. Some day I . . . I'm going to be a Royal."

"Ooooo," Seb C snickered, "a real Royal! Aren't we special!"

"I . . . uh . . . I'm not Royal yet. I guess it sort of takes time."

"Who cares?" Lyncher X questioned, momentarily diverting attention from the frightfully embarrassed Angus. And he was embarrassed, not only because of his royal-sounding names, but because he'd had no idea he was bigger than any of the other nestlings. But he was larger, quite a bit larger, and that surprised him. He was also surprised by their meanness, for he had never experienced meanness before— had not even imagined that it existed. Finally he was surprised that so many of the nestlings were covered with feathers—not pinfeathers like his own, but real feathers that were already showing the dark and mottled colors of the Sooty albatross. What was wrong with him, he wondered silently, that he was so underdeveloped.

27

"Well, you gonna just stand there looking dumb?" the voice of Lyncher X was suddenly growling at Angus, breaking his reverie. "Howie T says you wanted to go waddling today."

"I . . . I did. I mean, I do." And Angus, hurriedly stepping forward, found himself once again plowing a furrow in the sand with his bill.

There was a chorus of derisive laughter, Angus stumbled to his feet and managed two additional steps before falling again, and his doom was sealed. From that moment he was the butt of every joke that entered the minds of his Sooty fellows, and from that moment he was no longer Angus Austin.

"You ever seen anything so awkward?" Eleazor Dimfoddle snickered.

"Yeah," Lyncher X agreed with a sneer. "He is awkward. All bill, feet and butt. Hey! I don't think his second name should be Austin at all. I think it should be Awkward. Awkward fits him a whole lot better than Austin, wouldn't you say?"

28

"It fits him perfectly," the crowd chorused. "Awkward it is—Angus Awkward!"

"That is *not* my name!" Angus declared, his timid voice hardly rising above the laughing chorus of his fellows.

"He's so awkward he can't walk at all," A L hooted, ignoring Angus without difficulty.

"Or grow feathers," Seb C joined.

"Probably can't even paddle straight!" Eleazor Dimfoddle snickered.

"And if he ever gets any real, actual feathers, he'll still never get off the ground!" Lyncher X added merrily. "Nothing that big and awkward can possibly fly."

Suddenly Lyncher X started chanting, and quickly the whole flock of nestlings, Howie T included, were shrieking along.

> Ha ha, Angus Awkward
> Won't fly fast and low
> He can't even waddle good
> He's just too dumb and slow.

In humiliation Angus hung his head, too filled with the knowledge that they must be right to try a second time to stop them. And even as they were waddling away, chanting another stanza and howling in merriment, Angus could do nothing but mournfully agree.

29

> Ha ha, Angus Awkward
> Empty his belly is
> He'll never get good garbage
> But have to live on fizz.

Knowing they were right but still wondering why they were treating him the way they were, Angus made his painful, lonely way back toward the nest, hooking his way up the steep slope with his already sore bill, and thinking as he struggled how truly awkward he was.

And why was he so awkward? As the bedraggled albatross nestling thought of it, he suddenly realized that it had to be due to the squid. No one but him ate only squid, and no one but him was so big and awkward. The two had to be related!

Only, with a terrible lump in his throat, Angus realized that he could not do anything about it. He had made a promise to his mother that he couldn't break.

"Help me! Somebody please help me!"

Startled out of his reverie, Angus lifted his eyes and saw a nestling, a very young nestling, sprawled on the ground outside a high-mounded nest. Looking around, Angus saw that he was alone, and that there was nobody else to help the young bird.

"What's wrong?" he squawked as he waddled and fell and dragged himself closer. "You hurt or something?"

"I . . . I fell off the rim," the nestling responded, and then he burst into tears.

30

"Hey, don't cry." Angus's heart went out to this bird, and he knew he had to help him. "We'll get you back in your nest."

"We?"

"Well, I mean I will."

"How you gonna do it?" The nestling was doubtful. "You . . . you can hardly stand up yourself."

Angus was stumped. The small bird was right, of course. But there had to be a way he could help.

"I know. I'll squat down, and you get up on my back. Then I'll stand up, and you can waddle up my back and climb into your nest."

"But . . . you're so big, How will I ever get on top of you?"

"Hook onto my pinfeathers with your bill," Angus

declared as he squatted down. "Then just pull your-self up."

"Can I do that?" the nestling asked in amazement.

"Sure. That's part of what bills are for."

"And it won't hurt you?"

Angus hadn't thought of that, and suddenly he grew worried. It might hurt, it truly might. And he was getting awfully tired of pain. Still, this little nestling needed his help.

"Naw," he replied finally, "not much. Now go ahead, and let's get you back home again."

Doing as he was directed, the young bird dragged himself slowly onto Angus's back. And the nestling had been right about it hurting, Angus quickly dis-covered. In fact, it *really* hurt! But it had to be done, so he gritted his bill and endured, and after a long time the nestling gasped that he was securely in place.

"Okay," Angus grunted, "hold . . . on, while I stand up."

"Don't fall over," the nestling whined.

"I won't! Just you be ready."

Finally upright, Angus held his precarious balance while the nestling reached out and hooked the rim of his nest. Then he began dragging himself off Angus's back and onto the rim. And that, for some reason, was enough to upset Angus's balance.

"Hurry!" he gasped as he felt himself beginning to fall forward. "Pleeeease huuuurrrrrry."

"Don't fall," the nestling shrieked as he held des-perately with his bill.

"I . . . I can't help it!" Angus groaned. And he

31

couldn't, for in another second he had toppled forward and plowed another furrow in the sand with his sore, curved bill.

"Help!" the nestling shrieked from above, where it was now dangling from the rim of the nest by its bill. "Somebody, help me!"

"Use your feet," Angus mumbled through the sand on his bill as he struggled to right himself. "Don't just hang there! Use your feet!" He had to get back up again; he had to help.

"Use your feet to push, and your bill to pull! That's it. Now keep going."

"What's going on here?" a flying Sooty suddenly squawked from overhead. "What are you doing with my nestling, you big, ugly bird?"

Stunned, Angus cowered beneath the Sooty's dives. "I was . . . trying to help."

"You ninny!" the Sooty mother shrieked. "Instead of helping, you've nearly killed the poor little dear, dragging him out of the nest that way! I . . . I ought to have you dealt with, I should! Now get away! Go on! Shoo! I won't have someone as ugly and awkward as you trying to hurt my darling chick!"

And Angus, not knowing what else to say, turned and with broken heart made his way slowly and laboriously back to his own nest.

"Hey, Angus Awkward," another Sooty called from overhead, causing Angus to look up at the already-soaring bird, "when you try flying, let us know. Then we can all have a good laugh!" With a screech of mirth the Sooty glided away, and Angus

32

was more lonely and disconsolate than ever. Howie T and the others were right! He wasn't a Royal, and he could never be! All he was, was a big, dumb, awkward Sooty who deserved the name they had given him.

"Lyncher X and the others were certainly rude, weren't they?"

Spinning his head, Angus was surprised to see a young female nestling, an albatrix, making her way up the hill toward him. "It isn't rude if they're right," he responded as he dropped his gaze from her animated face.

"Then it was rude," she stated firmly as she stopped beside him. "Just as rude as that nestling's mother was, when all you were trying to do was help him. Hi. I'm Aura Lei. I saw what happened down at the beach, so I went after those rude albatri and gave them a piece of my mind. Especially that . . . that Lyncher X! Then I saw you trying to help —"

"You did *what* at the beach?" Angus asked, astounded.

"I told those nestlings that I thought they were a bunch of dodo birds, which is true as can be. I also gave that awful mother and her spoiled chick a piece of my mind! So, why didn't you wait and waddle back with me?"

Angus looked at her out of one round, round eye. "I can't even waddle by myself," he stated flatly. "Why should I want to make a fool of myself in front of someone else? Besides, how was I supposed to know about you? I haven't ever seen you in my life until now."

33

The young albatrix nestling giggled. "Good point." Then she climbed the side of Angus's nest and waited for him to follow. "Gosh, but you are big!" she said as Angus moved past her and slid down into his nest. "What does your mother feed you?"

"Why do you ask that?" Angus growled defensively.

"Actually, just to make conversation." Expertly Aura Lei hopped down inside the nest. "Already the whole colony is calling you Angus Awkward. Did you know that? You got famous in about two shakes of a short tailfeather!"

"Humph!"

34

"But I just told my parents you weren't really awkward at all. You were just uncoordinated because you got big so fast. I also told them that your real name is Angus Austin, which they think is a very regal name. So do I, by the way. Is it really what your mother feeds you that makes you so big?"

"You're pretty nosey."

Again the young nestling giggled. "I'll take out the word `nosey' and accept that as a compliment, for which I thank you sincerely. I'm glad you think I'm pretty. What is it she feeds you?"

"Squid. How come you don't have any feathers yet?"

Quickly Aura Lei looked down at herself. "Because I'm not very old yet, silly. What are squid?"

"They're . . . uh . . . they're . . . well, I don't know. They have lots of arms, I guess. Or legs. And they sure taste good, whatever they are. Mom gets them out in the ocean, far away from here, days and days away. She won't let me eat anything else."

"And that's what makes you so big?"

Angus shrugged, thinking while he did so that maybe this albatrix nestling wasn't so nosey after all. Just friendly. And very talkative. "I suppose so."

Cocking her head to one side, Aura Lei regarded him for a moment. "So," she finally asked, "why does she want you to be so big?"

"I don't know," Angus declared, actually chuckling a little at her forthright manner. "I guess she sort of thinks it'll give me understanding or something."

Aura Lei's eyes grew large. "Wow! That sounds wonderful. I wish I had understanding."

"How do you know you don't?"

Silently Aura Lei regarded her new friend. "I . . . I suppose I don't," she said thoughtfully. "But I haven't ever thought about it before."

"I probably wouldn't have either, if it hadn't been for the Royal."

Again Aura Lei looked puzzled. "What's a Royal?"

"You really don't know?"

"I don't think so, Angus Austin."

"Don't call me that! If you have to call me anything at all, just call me Gus. I like Gus."

The eyes of the young albatrix flashed with anger. "I will not call you that! Your name is Angus Austin, and that is who you should be. Now, are you going to tell me what a Royal is, or do I have to go ask some other bird?"

"Well," the big nestling declared, lowering himself

35

to a sitting position and doing his best to mimic his mother, "a Royal is practically the grandest and most wonderful sort of bird an albatross can ever be. His eyes are clear and bright and can see practically forever, his wings are long and sleek and white with fine black tips, and they are about twice as long as the longest Sooty wings in the whole colony."

"Serious?" Aura Lei looked amazed.

"It's the truth, all of it!" Angus found himself liking this albatrix more and more. "But there is more." And so he went on, excitedly describing the wondrous bird who had come to save his life—the bird he still found himself wishing he was.

And Aura Lei, listening with fascination, decided the same thing. "You know," she said thoughtfully after Angus had finished his description, "I think I want to grow up to be a Royal."

Angus looked cautiously at her. "You do?"

"Of course! Who wouldn't?"

"But . . . you can't! You . . . you're a Sooty!"

"Oh, fiddlededee!" Aura Lei was upset again, and if there had been anywhere for Angus to back away to, he would have done it in a second. Only, the nest was getting so small.

"My mother says a bird can be anything she wants to be, if she wants to be it badly enough! And my father agrees with her." Suddenly Aura Lei giggled. "Of course he doesn't dare disagree, either. My mother would pin his tailfeathers back if he did."

Angus nodded, though he had absolutely no idea what the young albatrix was talking about.

36

"Therefore," she concluded with her head held high, "I can become a Royal if I choose to. And I so choose!"

Instantly Angus decided she was right. "Well," he declared proudly, his confidence once again restored, "I know *I'm* going to be a Royal when I grow up, and that's for sure!"

"Then we'll be Royals together!" Aura Lei declared decisively, and she meant every word that she said.

This little albatrix...
was what others
called a reject,
a freak.

4

Once he had met Aura Lei, Angus was no longer so lonely. It wasn't so much that he spent time with her, as that other things seemed to change. For one thing, he quickly discovered that if he waddled anywhere near the shore, he would be certain to run into Lyncher X or one of his cronies, Howie T included. And once he had run into one of them, the name-calling and brow-beating would commence, and he would experience further degradation and humiliation.

To avoid that, which Angus wanted to do at all costs, he stayed at his nest a lot, learning all he could about the beauties of the sea and the sky, which never ceased to move him. And on the rare occasions when he left the nest, he either waddled up the hill and inland toward the cliffs that formed the backbone of his island, or on short ventures out among the nests of the other Sootys. And though the Sootys occasionally teased him and laughed at him, and though it seemed like he was always being called either Gus or Angus Awkward, he soon grew used to the names and even to accept them as a necessary part of his life.

Mostly, though, Angus was ignored. To the colony of Sootys, who were engrossed in keeping their own young warm or in wheeling and diving out in the bay in their never-ending quest to snatch the best of the worst offal from the flotsam and jetsam, the oversized young bird was little more than a momentary nuisance who waddled occasionally through the edges of their lives. Most of them simply didn't care about him one way or the other.

To his surprise, it didn't take Angus long to discover that he was not the only one so ignored. Here and there in the teeming colony were other misfits who in one way or another were as beaten up and lonely as himself. At first Angus avoided them as much as they seemed to avoid him. He had no specific reason for doing this, other than fear that even the misfits would turn against him and prove how truly awful he was.

But then one ordinary morning, all of that changed. As usual he was alone, watching the upper level winds drift cirrus clouds into the familiar mare's tails that signalled the distant approach of another storm. Angus was watching those clouds drift slowly into formation, and aching with the desire to be up there in the midst of them, drifting with them, when he became aware of soft whimperings in the sand and rocks somewhere nearby.

Looking around, he was amazed to see a young albatrix dragging herself laboriously along, not waddling, but literally pulling herself forward with her bill, much as he did as he climbed the side of his nest. But this bird wasn't climbing! She was simply moving forward, and each inch or two she gained apparently took all the strength and energy she could muster, for each effort brought forth the soft whimperings he had first heard.

But there was more. This little albatrix, like him, was what the others called a reject, a freak. Only her condition was far worse than his own. Severely deformed in body, she was a frightening sight, and for a moment Angus actually turned away, wondering as he did so whether her deformity was a pre-hatching condition or the result of some terrible injury. She was twisted grotesquely, she was gaunt to the point of starvation, she had obviously been pecked at by other birds, and she had only one eye. It was also obvious that she needed help, but as Angus looked at other nearby Sootys he realized that all of them were doing just as he was doing. They were completely ignoring her, pretending she didn't exist.

Of course Angus understood that she had been abandoned by her parents once they had discovered that her condition was hopeless, for that was the customary response of the Sootys to such things. Yet as he

40

watched the albatrix's pitiful efforts, Angus found his heart filling with compassion so great that he could not ignore it. She was alone, absolutely alone, and though nobody else was helping her, he had to try!

Taking a deep breath and putting aside his own fears and prejudices, Angus stumbled off his nest and made his way to her side. There he saw by the glazed look in her nearly closed eye that she was literally starving. Quickly regurgitating a little of the scanty contents of his own stomach, Angus lowered his head and worked his bill under her own, and there he held himself while she gasped and gagged and eventually managed to swallow a bite or two.

"Th . . . thank you."

"You're welcome," Angus responded, pushing his bill toward her again. And again she managed a couple of swallows.

41

"That . . . was wonderful," the chick gasped and panted. "I . . . haven't ever . . . eaten before."

Angus was too surprised by that to know how to respond, so he just kept pushing his bill at her until he was certain she could eat no more.

"Are . . . are you a Chosen One?" she gasped then.

"Me?" Angus snickered, abruptly forgetting his discomfort. "Not hardly. I'm just a nestling, like you. But I know a Chosen One. He helped my mom and me to stay alive for awhile."

"Is . . . that what Chosen Ones do?"

Angus nodded. "That's what my mom says."

"Then, why aren't you a Chosen One?"

The crippled little albatrix looked at Angus out of

her one round eye, and Angus, shocked by her reasoning, didn't know how to respond. He didn't feel like going into the issue of having to be a Royal, and he certainly didn't want to tell her what a complete putz he was. Besides, she obviously had a way of twisting logic until he couldn't argue with it, and she would probably try to do it again.

"What's your name?" he finally asked, deciding to change the subject altogether.

"N . . . name?" the emaciated albatrix replied weakly. "I . . . I don't have a name."

Angus was again shocked. "No name? Then let's change that! Everyone should have a name, don't you think?"

The small bird looked wonderingly at Angus. "I'm going to die," she said simply.

"So am I," Angus replied with a smile. "Maybe sooner than you. None of us knows. But I still have a name, and so shall you. That way we can be friends. Let's see. To me, you look like . . . like Leena Joy. That's it! Leena Joy. Do you like that name?"

Timidly the albatrix smiled. "Leena Joy," she breathed. "Does it fit me, do you think?"

"Of course it fits!" Angus's mind scrambled for an explanation. "You . . . uh . . . you're very lean, but you have so much joy in your eye that it's wonderful! So, Leena Joy fits you perfectly."

Slowly the starving, malformed albatrix did her best to smile. "Leena Joy," she breathed again. "That . . . that's beautiful!"

"Just like you," Angus declared sincerely, for it

42

was surely true that, in spite of her deformities, Leena Joy's smile of joy was beautiful.

"What . . . what's your name?"

"Gus," the bird replied quickly. Then, deciding to be honest and get the whole thing about himself out in the open immediately, he added, "Actually, my real name is Angus Austin, but a few call me Gus and most others call me Angus Awkward, on account of how big and ugly and ungainly I am."

"But . . . but that isn't true," the albatrix gasped, struggling to lift her head so that she could see Angus more clearly. "Why, I . . . I think you are magnificent, Angus Austin."

"Yeah," he responded, embarrassed. "Aura Lei says that, too. But I know better. Fact is, I'm not sure my bill will ever heal from digging furrows in the sand and rocks of this island every time I fall down."

43

"Aura Lei?"

Angus beamed. "Uh-huh. She's my best friend. Maybe she . . . well, maybe she's my chick, too, if you know what I mean."

"Goodness," Leena Joy breathed. "With a lovely name like that, I'll bet she's absolutely beautiful."

"She is," Angus agreed, then quickly added, "but in your own way, Leena Joy, you're just as beautiful as she is. Uh . . . where did you hatch out, and where were you trying to go?"

"I hatched out way over there, by the cliffs. When I realized that I had been left to die, I got to thinking about all that I couldn't see. The sound of the sea fascinated me the most, so I thought maybe I could make my way to the shore, and maybe even feel the waves wash in and over me." The albatrix was suddenly embarrassed. "I . . . I don't know if I can paddle much, but even if I can't, I'd like to see the waves come in, and just once feel the freedom of their power."

"I've felt it," Angus said, a faraway look in his eyes, "and it is wonderful or frightening, depending on whether or not a storm is here. Did you know the waves are usually green, Leena Joy, though depending on the light they can range from dark blue-green to practically black? And of course there is all sorts of white foam where they crash in, not only riding the crests of the waves, but running in thin lines down their sheer faces and gathering in clumps that get pushed ahead of the swells. But the most beautiful sight of all, at least in my opinion, is to squat on the shore just before sunset and watch the sun through the sheer walls of the waves. I'm telling you, Leena Joy, it's absolutely impossible to imagine the color! My mother says the water bends the sunlight into the colors I can see, and I guess she's right. All I know is, it's beautiful."

"Oh, Angus Austin, I'll just bet it is! Before I die I would so like to see such a thing for myself."

"You will, Leena Joy. In fact, if you'd like I'll take you there."

Angus rose to start out, and with a smile Leena Joy stopped him. "Not now, Angus. I . . . I'm too tired. Maybe if I rest a little while?"

Instantly amenable, Angus squatted back down

44

and began visiting again. For hours he and Leena Joy talked, not of anything special, but just of this and that. He spoke to her of other aspects of the sea and the sky and of his yearning to be a part of them. He grumbled about Lyncher X and his other tormentors. And he talked endlessly about Aura Lei, wishing all the while that the lovely albatrix would come by so he could introduce her to Leena Joy. And he even grumbled about the squid his mother had made him promise to eat, and of how it was turning him into a huge, awkward monster.

Finally, when it was nearly dark, Angus helped the emaciated chick to the base of his nest, where he hollowed out a bit of sand as a temporary abode for her.

"Is it really okay if I stay here?" she asked timidly.

"Of course it is. I'd take you into my nest if I knew how to get you there."

Leena Joy giggled. "I have that same problem, Angus Austin."

"Yeah, I imagine. Do . . . do you really think you're dying?"

Her one eye open wide, the young bird did her best to nod. "Yes. And very soon, too."

"Tonight?" Angus was suddenly nervous.

"Oh, I don't think so," she replied, and Angus could see that she was trying to put him at ease. "But maybe it will be tomorrow, or the next day. I suppose it depends on when I can get to the sea."

"Are . . . you afraid?"

"Of dying?" Leena Joy's one eye sparkled. "Oh, no! The Creator has promised me that when I die I will be

45

free, just like the waves, or the birds in our colony when they soar far and farther and high and higher until I can't even see them anymore. Only I will go even farther and higher than that, and have more freedom than them all."

"You've talked with the . . . the Creator?"

"Why, yes. Many times. Why?"

"I . . . uh . . . I didn't know the Creator could talk with . . . well, us, I guess."

"If He has the power to be our Creator," Leena Joy asked gently, "then don't you suppose He also has the power to talk with us?"

Angus had never thought of it that way, and once again Leena Joy's strange logic surprised him. "I . . . guess so. I just . . . well, He hasn't ever spoken to me."

46

Leena Joy was serious. "Have you ever spoken with Him? Or asked Him something?"

Feeling foolish, Angus shook his head that he had not.

"Then maybe that's why." Slowly Leena Joy's eye dropped closed. Then, as if with great effort, she opened it again. "I . . . I'm tired, Angus Austin. Maybe we could talk again . . . tomorrow?"

Before Angus could even answer, Leena Joy was asleep. For a moment the big nestling watched her, wondering, thinking. Then he crept quietly up to his nest, where for hours he remained awake thinking of the tiny deformed bird who lay below. Over and over he rehearsed as much of their conversation as he could remember, savoring the insights and storing them in his memory.

He also thought of the severe deformities with which Leena Joy was afflicted, and it amazed him that her twisted body seemed to mean nothing to her, nothing at all. She appeared not the least bit ashamed of herself. And strangely, he didn't feel embarrassed for her, either. She was beautiful in every way possible, and her joyful countenance radiated love every bit as much as his mother's when she looked at him. Truly Leena Joy was a remarkable bird, and Angus sensed that she had somehow managed to return far more to him than he had given her.

But most of all, Angus found himself worrying that in the morning she would be dead and he would have no chance to get her to the sea. For she was dying, and Angus knew it. He had been rather flippant with her about his own future death, but now he found himself wondering if he would handle dying as well as she. Probably not, for he certainly had no such understanding of the Creator—or from Him—as did Leena Joy. It was interesting, for now that he thought of it, he knew his mother had such a knowledge, for she had somehow enticed the Creator into sending their Royal Chosen One to them. But could gaining such a knowledge be as simple as the tiny albatrix had suggested? After all, what could be more simple than to talk to the Creator? What, indeed!

"O, great Creator," he breathed in a first, halting, and very uncomfortable attempt at communication with the divine, "I . . . I'm not asking anything for me. But could you help this crippled albatrix . . . I mean, Leena Joy, to see and feel the sea? I think that would

47

make her happy. So, if you could please keep her alive until I can get her there . . ."

In the morning Angus overslept, and when he got to Leena Joy's place of rest she was gone. Following after her as best he could without a lot of falling, Angus was overjoyed to find her lying peacefully on the beach, with Aura Lei squatted beside her.

"Leena Joy wanted to be here early," Aura Lei stated simply as Angus waddled up. "She wanted to see the ocean like you described it, only at sunrise."

"And it's beautiful!" Leena Joy breathed happily. "Simply beautiful!"

"But . . . how did you know her?" Angus pressed of Aura Lei, too dumbfounded yet to see the glories of the new day.

48   Aura Lei smiled sweetly. "I came to see you, Angus Austin, but you were asleep. As I was leaving, I found Leena Joy struggling along toward the shore. Of course I couldn't just leave her like that, so while I was helping her, your name somehow came up. She told me all about your visit last night. I'm glad that you were so sweet to her."

"Well," Angus stated uncomfortably, "I didn't do much. Fed her a little is all."

"You gave her a lovely name."

"Oh, yeah. It . . . it . . . well, it fits her."

For a moment Angus stood in silence beside the two albatrixes, wondering that the clamoring of the morning colony could be so drowned by the muted thunder of the sea. He wondered too at the clear morning light that danced off the tops of the distant, choppy waves. Everything around him was so beautiful, so amazing, that just the sight of it thrilled him to the very depths of his soul. In fact it still brought tears of joy to his round, round eyes, tears that seemed to come often, and which he tried desperately to hide from Aura Lei.

But turning away from her to do so, Angus noticed for the first time the expression of ecstasy on the countenance of Leena Joy, and he forgot all about hiding his tears. In amazement he watched the tiny albatrix nestling revel as the low and somehow cleansing waves washed over her, and for a time he forgot even that he was with Aura Lei. Instead he could think only of Leena Joy, and of the pure happiness it was so obvious she was feeling. It was as if it didn't even matter to her that nature had played such a terrible trick. In fact, Angus couldn't escape the feeling that her deformities had all been part of some much larger, divine plan—a plan that she had long before taken part in formulating.

49

"Aura Lei," the physically crippled albatrix said abruptly, breaking into Angus's thoughts, "thank you for helping me to see all this. And to feel it. It is all so gorgeous that I can't even begin to take it all in."

"You're very welcome," Aura Lei responded softly.

"You know, you're even more beautiful than I had imagined when Angus Austin told me about you."

Aura Lei was embarrassed, but if Leena Joy noticed, she gave no sign. She simply smiled her crooked smile, and then turned to Angus, her countenance still radiating her peaceful happiness.

"Thank you, Angus Austin, for being my friend— my Chosen One. Thank you for describing for me the beauties of our world. And . . . and thank you for helping me to feel . . . to feel . . . ready."

"Ready for what?" Angus asked, not understanding. And only when the tiny albatrix didn't respond did Angus realize that Leena Joy's spirit had risen and slipped through the doorway of immortality, and was already gliding easily away,going high and higher, far and farther, returning in perfection to the presence of the great Creator. He couldn't actually see her, but somehow he knew that was exactly what she was doing, where she was going. And the knowledge gave him a tiny bit of peace.

50

In the days and weeks that followed, though he and Aura Lei seldom spoke of her, Angus came to understand that Leena Joy had added immeasurably to his soul. More, he felt that her passing had torn a hole within him, a hole of loneliness and sorrow mixed with the sweet pleasure of having known her, that he knew he would never wish to be filled.

...The brightest spots in Angus'
life... were the frequent visits of
the rapidly maturing
Aura Lei...

5

Leena Joy had changed Angus in another way, too.
Oh, he remained timid and afraid of association with
the other Sootys of the colony. And primarily because
of their persecution, his assessment of his big and
awkward self did not change much. But for the remainder of that mostly lonely summer, whenever he
encountered another bird who was in one way or another a misfit, he found some way of reaching out. He
looked at them, he saw their suffering and loneliness
rather than their differences, and he was so reminded
of Leena Joy and himself that his heart seemed to
open up to them of its own accord.

Of course none of the things he did for them were
what he thought of as a big deal, and not for a mo-

ment did Angus even suppose that he was doing any-thing extraordinary. Instead, he was simply being the sort of friend he wished that he had. And because he thought so much of her, he was constantly inviting his treasured Aura Lei to do the same.

And she *was* treasured. In fact, the brightest spots of all in Angus's life that summer were the frequent visits of the rapidly maturing Aura Lei. Yet she never spoke of her own developing maturity, but always spoke of him, in every way possible encouraging him to "find his understanding," as she had heard his mother put it.

"But how am I supposed to do that, Aura Lei?" he asked one rainy and dismal afternoon in early fall. "What can possibly be the understanding of an over-grown gooneybird who can't even fly?"

52

"I don't know, Angus Austin," Aura Lei responded kindly after clicking against his bill with hers, "but that is because it is not my particular understanding. It is yours, and so it is up to you to find it."

Angus loved clicking bills with her, which is very much like kissing in other species, and so he repeated the action, sometimes again and again. "I'm glad you're here," he sighed, looking down at her. "It makes me want to keep trying, and not give up."

"You shouldn't need me for that," Aura Lei scolded tenderly.

"Yeah," Angus sighed, "I know. Only—"

"Only nothing! Think of Leena Joy! Think of all the other birds who have become your friends! And think of yourself, Angus Austin. Why, you're the finest, strongest bird in the entire colony!"

At that Angus snickered, and Aura Lei grew more vehement than ever. "I mean it! Sometimes when I look at you I am almost frightened, thinking of the greatness that lies in your heart. In fact, I find myself wondering that I am actually here in your nest with you, talking with you. Other times," and Aura Lei dropped her head a little with embarrassment, "I think I am envious of you."

"Envious?" Angus questioned with surprise. "What on earth for?"

"Because . . . because of the rearing you have received from your mother. Because of the love it is so obvious she has for you. Because of the love that you have for others. And . . . I guess a little because I know what a fine Royal you will one day be . . . and I am afraid I will miss out on that."

53

"I'll never be a Royal and you know it!" Angus responded, cocking his head to one side like Aura Lei did and fixing her with his round, round eye. "I'm a Sooty, just like you and every other bird in this colony. Besides, why should you miss out on anything? If I can someday be great, then you can surely be greater. Why, you're normal, Aura Lei! You don't ever have to worry about being a big, awkward freak. You don't ever have to worry about being ridiculed by your friends. You don't even have to worry about starving to death. You have everything I've always dreamed of having!"

"Yes, Angus Austin," Aura Lei admitted sadly, "I do. And compared to what you have been given, what I have is worth practically nothing. Oh, Angus Austin, can't you see? You have been chosen! You have been given a gift that is more precious than anything either of us can even begin to imagine."

"What gift? My size?"

"No, silly. Your heart! You have a Royal heart! Time and again I've seen love and compassion in your eyes as you've helped others who struggle and suffer. And I love how just seeing the beauties of the sky and sea can make you cry."

"I only cry because I'm a big booby," he replied softly.

"You are not. You're wonderful! And in spite of my silly envy, I am so proud and happy for you that it makes *me* cry! Don't give up on yourself, Angus Austin. Please don't give up on finding your understanding. Not just for your mom's sake, but for mine. Please, Angus Austin."

54

...Angus could feel himself going upward,... upward and... going over sideways and backward, tipping and falling, faster and faster...

6

Gradually the sun moved northward and hung lower in the sky, the hazy days of fall turned colder, and one by one the Sooty nestlings who were Angus's age caught the wind beneath their wings and took flight. Though he was glad to see them go, for their persecution of him had never let up but had only grown worse since that terrible day on the beach, Angus was also envious. With all his big and tender heart he longed to leave the earth and soar into the far and distant sky. Only, he was still molting, and still producing feathers that would never support a bird of his size. Worse, his mother's absences were growing longer and longer, for the squid were getting increasingly difficult to find. Thus, though Angus continued to grow, he was looking more and more scrawny, his eyes were getting more hollow, and his hunger seemed never to be satisfied.

As May crept into June the icy blasts of the Antarctic winter shut down the cannery ship and the trawlers, which all sailed away northward taking their awful offal with them. Soon after that the cold and lack of offal amid the flotsam and jetsam drove away the remaining occupants of the albatross colony—all, that is, but Aura Lei and a shivering, bedraggled Angus Austin. And he couldn't leave because he did not yet have the feathers required to lift his huge and awkward body into flight.

"They were right!" he thought night after lonely night as he tried to get his huge body airborne when none of the others could see his crashing falls. "My name *should* have been Awkward. Angus Awkward, the flightless gooneybird!" And in frustration and shame he returned again and again to his tiny, lonely nest.

Then came the day when even Aura Lei, with tears of sadness, clicked bills with Angus for the last time. "I . . . I'm sorry," she whispered as she preened a useless pinfeather from his huge but scrawny chest, "but I must leave you, Angus Austin. Something is . . . is calling me, and I must go."

"Don't cry, Aura Lei," Angus whispered, blinking back tears of his own. "I know the feeling, and I'd go too, if I could."

"Will . . . will you promise to come and find me?"

Taking a deep breath, Angus nodded. "You bet I

will! You've always been the best to me, Aura Lei, even when everyone else was . . . well, you know how they've been. Anyway, I'll miss you. Tons! But I hope you find what's calling you, and I hope it makes you happy."

Aura Lei smiled through more tears. "Thank you, Angus Austin. I will miss you, too, more than you can know. And I . . . I will never forget you."

With that she was in the air and gone, and Angus was truly alone on the rocky, windswept island, doing his best to remain warm as he waited for the increasingly rare visits from his mother.

Oh how he longed to fly, to lift off and sail after his beloved Aura Lei. Far off in the northwest the setting sun was painting a path of crimson light, beckoning him away across the jeweled sea. On the cliffs above him, clumps of dried grass shifted uneasily and then reluctantly bent before the freshening wind, their every whisper encouraging him to go.

57

Why, he asked himself as he stretched his useless wings in another futile attempt at liftoff, had he been hatched to be so different? Why had his mother insisted that he promise to avoid the garbage everyone else was allowed to eat—the garbage that would have made him just like them? And why, most of all, had he been dumb enough to make such a promise in the first place?

But he had, he reminded himself with a fierce click of his bill, and he would remain a bird of his word, no matter what else he was called upon to suffer!

And then came a day in mid-winter, after his

mother had been gone more than two weeks, when the sun didn't even show itself above the northern horizon, and the darkness only half-lifted from the craggy face of Angus's lonely island. It was a day when the wind seemed more fierce than normal, and when a brief flurry of snow raced horizontally past the shivering young albatross, not even pausing to cover the rocks and hollows that had once been nests to the colony of Sootys. In short, it was a day when Angus was practically sure that he was dying.

"Mom!" he shrieked into the storm, "where are you?"

Straining, Angus could hear nothing but the wind. But she had to be out there, he reasoned. She just had to be! In all his life she had never let him down, had never failed him. Surely she would be coming for him now.

"Mom!" he wailed desperately. "Mother, I can't stay alive much longer."

"She can't hear you, Angus Austin."

In surprise Angus looked up to see the big Royal glide to a landing on the rocks above him. Only, for some reason he didn't seem quite so big as he had a few months earlier.

"Angus Austin, this time your mother won't be coming back."

"What? But why?"

"Because that is the law of the Creator. You're now large enough to live life on your own. So you must."

"But . . . I haven't eaten in more than two weeks! If she doesn't come back, then I'll surely die."

"I doubt that," the Royal responded, smiling in spite of Angus's obvious distress. "But you will lose enough weight that flight will come more easily. Remember, it's warmer where the sun shines."

And to Angus's gape-billed amazement, the Royal lifted from the rock and vanished into a thick swirl of snow.

For a moment he didn't know what to do. He was alone again, totally alone, and the realization literally took his breath away. Though he could hardly believe it, not only was the Royal gone, but now Angus knew that his mother would not be coming back!

Blankly he stared toward the distant horizon where last he had seen her, having no idea whatsoever about what he should do next. "Mom!" he shrieked again into the gale-force winds that tore down the slope of his island. "Mom! You can't leave me yet! You just can't! I'll starve to death." Angus paused, and his only reply was the howling of the wind as it picked up a knot or two in speed. "You know I can't fly, Mom," he cried, feeling incredibly desperate. "I . . . I'm too big, too awkward, and I just keep molting these useless little feathers."

There was no answer, and though he had expected none, Angus was nonetheless hurt and even more lonely. Why would his mother leave him, he wondered? Why would she go now, at the very worst possible time? If she wasn't bringing him squid any longer, how would he eat? There was not even any garbage in the bay for him to paddle out to. Worse, there was no other living creature on the island, no

59

one to help him or even to talk with him. He was absolutely alone.

"*Moooootherrrr*," he wailed then, his heart filled with grief. "I can't stand it any more! First all the Sootys left, then Aura Lei, and now you! Why, Mom? Why did you leave me? I can't stand being alone, I tell you! I don't even want to live anymore! I mean it, Mom! It just isn't worth it!"

Casting about with his eyes to see if perchance his mother had returned to hear his pleadings, Angus suddenly realized that he had never been to the crest of the island, to the high point of rocks where he might see the other side. And for the first time in his short life he began to wonder if he was really as alone as he had always thought. Why, on the other side there might be another colony of albatri, birds he could speak with and maybe even get something to eat from. All he had to do was get himself up to the top, where he could take a long, long look at the other side.

Suiting thought to action Angus waddled out of his earthen nest and, by hooking onto rocks and tufts of grass with his bill, gradually pulled himself upward. The rocky pinnacle above him seemed a long way off, and Angus did not make very steady progress as he dragged himself toward it. Not only was gravity and the ferocious wind against him, but he had eaten nothing in so long that he was considerably weakened by the fast. Still he pressed on, his determination driven by desperation as he used his ungainly wings to thrust against the sand and rocks,

thereby balancing himself while his bill pulled upward and his wide feet waddled after.

He did not know how long it took him to make the
climb; in fact after a time he wasn't certain if he re-
membered ever doing anything else. In his mind the
rocky point became a monster of unimaginable pro-
portions, a behemoth whose steep sides were absolutely unscalable. Yet Angus persisted, simply because he no longer had the strength to realize he
could stop and turn back.

And thus, in a moment when he least expected it,
the young bird somehow scaled the last, steep cliffs
and arrived at the top—and was nearly knocked end
over tailfeathers back down by the terrible force of
the wind.

"Omasquawk!" he gasped as he squinted his eyes
and braced himself against the howling gale. "Mom!
Or anybody else, for that matter! Even you, Royal!
Hey! Is there anyone down there who can hear me?"

Realizing at length that the wind was blowing his
cries back into his face, Angus lowered his head,
closed his bill, squinted his eyes, and glared down the
slope before him. He was looking for signs of life, for
anything that would relieve his loneliness. But alas,
the other side of Angus's island looked even more
barren than the side on which he lived, and now the
poor young albatross was forced to acknowledge that
he was truly alone.

"Mother!" he squawked as he lifted his head again.
"Please, Mom."

At that instant a terrible gust of wind, at least

double in velocity what Angus had already been facing, ripped up the slope and slammed into his weakened body. With a screech of fear Angus felt himself pummeled backward, straight toward the edge of the cliff he had so miraculously climbed. Awkwardly he struggled to get his wide webbed feet braced beneath him, and to crouch down against the wind, his neck outstretched and his head low. Still he slid backward, slowly, inexorably, inching toward the cliff and to what would most certainly be a horrid, painful death on the rocks below.

"Moooooootherrrrrrrr," he wailed pitifully, and then another horrendous gust of wind slammed against him, tipping him backward and almost toppling him over and off the cliff. In terror he closed his eyes and reached out with his wings, instinctively seeking to regain his balance. But he couldn't! Instead he was pulled and lifted even more! With his pounding heart caught in his constricted throat Angus could feel himself going upward, upward, his reaching feet finally being lifted from the cold surface of the rock. And then with a feeling of horror he felt himself going over sideways and backward, tipping and falling, faster and faster.

"Omasquawk!" he screamed. "Omasquaaaaaaaawk."

When he didn't immediately slam into the waiting rocks, Angus felt only bewilderment. Of course, his benumbed mind reasoned, he must have climbed higher than he had thought. But then, when another agonizing eternity had passed and there was still no bone-shattering impact, Angus forced open one of his

62

eyes. And discovered, to his dumbfounded amazement, that he was flying!

He was flying! He, Angus who was called Awkward, the one who was too big to ever get airborne, was actually flying! He was sailing with the wind! Well, not with it, exactly, but across it, skipping along on the howling currents of air as if it were the most natural thing in the world for him to be doing.

He was flying!

And then Angus chanced to look downward, and instantly his panic returned. There was no island below him! There was nothing but heaving waves and flying spray being carried, like him, before the wind.

"Mom," he yelped again, for he truly knew of no one else to call, and then he tried to turn back toward the island. Immediately he found himself two hundred feet higher than he had been before, and still climbing so fast it was taking his breath away!

63

"Omasquawk," he yelped, turning with the wind again, and then he was hurtling along as before, only higher, riding the ferocious air currents that had blown him off his rocky home. But at least, he thought with a sigh of relief as he tilted his wings only slightly this time, he wasn't climbing anymore. And neither was he falling, which knowledge gave the young albatross an even greater feeling of relief.

Carefully then he flew across the wind, tilting his long primaries first on his left wing and then on his right, and exuberantly discovering what each accomplished. Next he tucked his wings, yelped with fear when he dropped like a rock, and almost groaned with relief when by outstretching his wings again he stopped his fall.

There was more Angus could experiment with—his tailfeathers, the secondaries under his wings close to his body, his angle of wing-tilt, even the uses of the wind. It wasn't long, therefore, before he stopped thinking of the wind as a terribly frigid gale, a horrible storm that had carried him from his home. Rather he was beginning to see it as something to ride, almost a game to be played, as he finally began the process of seeking out his understanding.

64

Angus Austin did nothing but ride the winds of the "Roaring Forties"...

7

For the next several months Angus Austin did nothing but ride the winds of the "Roaring Forties," the region between 40 and 50 degrees latitude. He was not interested in following the regular migratory routes of the albatross; he was not even interested in finding Aura Lei. What he *was* interested in was food, plenty of it, and he quickly discovered that it was not as easy to come by as he had supposed.

Often he would go days and days between meals, simply because he could find nothing to eat. Partly that was because the seas were usually stormy, and partly it was because Angus had a tendency to let the winds lift him so high that he could not see the food he craved. And though he knew that was a problem, the young albatross simply could not control his flight well enough to stay lower. Whenever he got down low enough to see what he was looking for, he would stall out and splash. Every time!

Still, while he was taking his rare rests on the water Angus occasionally stumbled into schools of squid, which he ate ravenously, and once in a while he actually managed to hook a few small fish with his bill, which were not as tasty, but which helped fill the hollow that was always within him. Thus, at the very least, he kept himself alive.

Day after day Angus flew, stretching wide his long, thin, airfoil-like wings and fleeing eastward through the beautiful sky before the prevailing westerlies. Skirting the Cape of Good Hope he winged northward past Madagascar and the Mascarene Islands in the Indian Ocean. Roughly following the Tropic of Capricorn he continued east until it was necessary to veer south at Cape Inscription on Australia's west coast, after which he rode the winds completely around the land of Down Under, and then turned north to sail over the Tasman Sea. Eastward the lonely albatross continued, over the Kermadec and Tubuai Islands, past Bora Bora, Tahiti and the Pitcairn Islands, and on past solitary Easter Island with its strange basaltic carvings.

Veering south again at the Juan Fernandez Islands, Angus followed the Drake Passage through the Scotia Sea past Cape Horn and the Falklands and on across the great South Atlantic until in almost no time, it seemed, he was back at the Cape of Good Hope. The

66

wandering bird had thus completely circumnavigated the globe, which surprised him beyond measure.

Angus even found himself enjoying the solitude of his lonely life, blanking his mind and simply enjoying the sensation of flight. The trouble was, despite the fact that by nature he was a perfect aviator, riding before even the most severe storms with ease and grace, he knew absolutely that he was awkward, and that it was not possible to learn the fundamentals of low-level flight.

Still, except for the never-ending hunger his life was good, and—

"Well, if it isn't my young friend, Angus Austin."

Almost tumbling over in surprise, Angus was startled to discover that he was not flying alone. A gleaming white Royal was flying just above and behind his right wingtip, matching perfectly his every move.

"You?" Angus declared, his mind reeling with a joy that he wasn't sure he wanted to feel. "Why do you keep showing up in my life?"

The Royal chuckled. "Perhaps it is because I choose to. But I am pleased that you continue to recognize me."

"Well, actually I'm happy to see you," Angus responded, not knowing exactly what else to say to this bird who had so changed his life.

"You seem to be developing into a fine feather of an albatross," the Royal declared, sounding pleased. "But you look terribly scrawny. Aren't you eating properly?"

"Properly? Who knows about properly? I count my blessings when I can find anything to eat at all."

The Royal chuckled. "Maybe that's because you're flying too high."

"I know," Angus agreed with a sigh. "But when I get low enough to see the schools of squid, I stall out and splash."

"Hmmm," the Royal mused thoughtfully. "Do you know what an ellipse is?"

Slowly Angus shook his head.

"It is an oblong circle, almost an oval. To fly low and slow, where you can see the squid schooling to the surface and get quickly to them, you need to fly in an ellipse. Follow me, Angus Austin, and I'll show you how to do it."

68   And so Angus learned the art of flying low and slow, and of expending minimal energy to accomplish it. He had known for a long time that wind velocity was significantly lower near the waves than it was a few meters up, for that was always where he stalled out and splashed. But abruptly he discovered that not only was it unnecessary to stall near the water, but in fact the lower, slower air was a positive thing to be used. To do so, the big Royal taught him to enter a fast downwind glide beginning up where the wind velocity was higher. This gave Angus considerable speed with only a small loss of altitude. As he reached maximum speed at the top of the slower layer of air he was taught to turn cross-wind, briefly skimming the waves and moving even lower.

Then the Royal showed Angus how to turn again,

this time into the wind. And because he was still moving at such a good speed, he could remain in the lower, slower air for a long, level glide. He could maintain a very low altitude and only slowly lose speed, meanwhile searching easily for the surface-schooling squid. Finally, when his air-speed reached a critical low, Angus was taught to turn cross-wind and be lifted in a short, steep climb, taking him once again into the faster air. And there, his ellipse completed, he could turn once again and glide downwind, gaining fresh momentum and beginning a whole new ellipse.

More remarkably, while he reached speeds of fifty to seventy miles an hour on the downward legs of his ellipses, Angus soon learned that he could go literally hours and even days with never a flap of his long, narrow wings. Of course on the days when there was no wind, or in the areas where winds seldom blew, flight became terribly burdensome. So Angus was also shown by the Royal how to avoid such areas, and how to conserve his energy by resting on the sea when calm days did occur, feeding as he could and waiting for the almost certain winds of early evening to once again lift him into the air.

It was an exhilarating time for Angus, and he was just starting to enjoy the almost silent companionship of the gleaming Royal when he awoke one fall morning, midst the undulating waves where they had been sleeping, to find the gleaming black and white bird gone again. At first upset, Angus soon reconciled to the rare bird's departure, and continued in his own

69

lonely way. But with the things he had been taught he was no longer so hungry, and he felt very grateful for that.

The years passed quickly after that, with Angus Austin flying and learning and continuing on his solitary way, relentlessly seeking the understanding that his mother had counseled him to find, but always failing to find it. And then one day when he was well into his fourth summer, strictly by chance Angus flew over a small island that seemed somehow familiar.

"Omasquawk!" he suddenly shouted to the wind, "that's my island! That's where I was hatched out! And look, the colony's filled with albatri again. Maybe those are my friends down there. Maybe . . . maybe . . . I'm going down!" And circling lower and lower, Angus pulled up and made a rather awkward landing on the pebbly beach.

"Who is the wide-body?" a bird called from a nearby nest.

"I don't know," another shouted, "but I definitely felt the ground shake."

There was a chorus of laughter and other remarks about the big, awkward gooneybird, and then from out in the water a voice called, "Hey, Gus, is that you?"

"Howie T?" Angus responded, looking toward the sea.

"Yeah," the Sooty replied as he flapped toward the beach. "You know, I thought you were dead. And maybe you are," he added as he waddled ashore. "You're looking awful pale, Gus. What sort of an albatross are you?"

70

"Aw, I keep molting these goofy-colored gray feathers," Angus responded, feeling embarrassed. "I think it's just a phase. So . . . uh . . . what's happening here?"

"Not much," Howie T replied as he squirted some oil onto his Sooty feathers and began to preen. "The old birds are all back nesting. But me and the guys, well, we just dropped by to check out the chicks, if you know what I mean."

"Uh . . . yeah." Actually Angus had no idea why Howie T and the others would want to check out the new nestlings, but neither was he foolish enough to open his bill and say so. If he didn't have understanding, in his four years of life he had at least learned a few things.

"Listen, Howie T," he asked abruptly, "have you seen my mom around?"

"No," the Sooty said with a shake of his head, "I haven't seen her. But then I haven't been up by the nests, either. I'm having too much of a blast clicking bills and dancing with the chicks down here on the beach. Listen, Gus, I've got to waddle. Somebody cute, you know." Howie T winked knowingly. "Maybe later?"

Angus nodded, relieved that Howie T was leaving, and having no intention whatsoever of seeking him out later. After all, he could still remember the rudeness the bird and his buddies had shown him in years past. Besides, right now what he wanted most of all was to see if his mother—

"Hello, Angus Austin."

Looking up, Angus was surprised to see a young albatrix standing a little way off, smiling at him. But what was even more surprising was that she was not wearing the mottled Sooty plumage of the other albatri in the colony. Instead she was feathered with almost the same light color of gray as himself.

"H . . . hello," he stammered, not knowing what else to say.

"You don't remember me, do you?" The albatrix was waddling closer, and Angus was suddenly having trouble breathing.

"I'm Aura Lei, Angus Austin." She was now very close, and he was starting to sweat oil from his bill he was so nervous. "Don't you remember me?"

"A . . . Aura Lei?" he managed to squeak.

72

"That's right." Aura Lei reached up and tenderly clicked his bill—once, twice, three times. And abruptly Angus was beyond nervousness and was certain he had just died and gone to heaven, just as Leena Joy had once done. If this was really Aura Lei, he was thinking, then—

"You *do* remember me, don't you?"

"Omasquawk! I'll say I do!"

Smiling, Aura Lei reached up and clicked his bill again, and Angus nearly lost his balance and fell over he was so ecstatic.

"I'm so happy to see you, Angus Austin! When I left you, I was truly afraid that you might die. I didn't want to leave, either, but I just couldn't seem to stop myself. But I've never stopped thinking about you."

"Really?"

"Of course not!" Aura Lei smiled brightly. "Now, tell me about you. Where have you been, and what have you been doing?"

Angus shrugged self-consciously. "Just flying, I guess, and eating. You know, the usual things."

"But you didn't follow our migratory route up the western coast of South America, did you? I mean, that's where I was, following the wonderfully rich currents of the Pacific Ocean, and I certainly never saw you."

"No, I didn't go there, Aura Lei. I just sort of drifted before the winds, trying to stay alive. I guess I've been around the world twice by now."

"You have?" The albatrix was awed.

"Yeah. It isn't that hard. You just keep ahead of the winds, do your best to keep water under you, and pretty soon you've been around the world."

73

"Maybe you've become a Wandering Albatross," Aura Lei teased.

"I doubt it," Angus replied with a chuckle. "Actually, Aura Lei, I'm a Sooty just like everybody else, except that all the squid I ate when I was a nestling made me big; and now I keep molting these weird gray feathers."

"I . . . uh . . . mine are the same." Aura Lei was suddenly self-conscious.

"Yeah, I noticed." Angus knew his huge webbed foot was in his bill all the way to the feathers, and he felt terribly embarrassed. "But on you they look good!" he added lamely.

"They look good on you, too, Angus Austin. And I don't think you should call them weird, either."

"Gus," the albatross Howie T gasped, suddenly appearing from behind some rocks, "you gotta get outa here, bird!"

"What? But—"

"It's Lyncher Xenophobe! You remember—the meanest bird in the colony? He and his gang are coming, and they're mad, Gus! Mad! Take off! Hurry, before Lyncher X plucks you alive!"

Angus was stunned. Worse, he could feel his heart hammering with fear. Of all the nestlings who had once taunted him and made his life miserable, the one called Lyncher X had been far and away the worst. And his buddies had not been far behind. Now they were all coming back?

Quickly Angus looked around, searching for a stretch of level sand he could use for a takeoff.

"Say! Who is the big lummox with my chick?"

With a gulp of fear, Angus realized that he was too late, and that, no matter what he did, he could not escape in time. It was Lyncher X, all right. Angus would have recognized his voice anywhere, and avoided it every time.

"I asked," the harsh voice snarled from behind him, "who the major freak is whose been billing my albatrix?"

Turning and looking downward at the angry bird, Angus realized with a sinking, empty feeling that in four years nothing had changed, and that he was in for more of the old tormenting.

"You . . . your albatrix?" Angus gulped, his voice

74

squeaking. "I . . . I didn't know, Lyncher X. Honest. I just got back, and—"

"Oh, no!" Lyncher X groaned while the crowd of his Sooty buddies grouped behind him, snickering. "Don't tell me it's Angus Awkward, the jumbo-bird reject. I thought we were rid of you for good."

"I . . . uh . . . I just—"

"Listen, you clumsy oaf, you don't squawk unless you're invited. Hear me? And you *definitely* don't mess with my chick—not with bills, not even with squawking!"

"Yeah," Eleazor Dimfoddle added. "Now, beat it!"

Feeling absolutely humiliated, Angus mumbled some sort of apology and started to back away. All he wanted was to disappear completely, to become non-existent so that Aura Lei wouldn't see him, wouldn't even know him.

"Angus Austin, where are you going?" The alba-trix's voice sounded desperate.

"I . . . uh . . . I didn't mean to intrude, Aura Lei. I'm sorry."

"I'm not Lyncher X's chick, you foolish bird!" Aura Lei was so angry she stamped her webbed foot. "In fact, I don't even like the egotistical creep, and I've told him to stop bothering me."

"You have? I mean . . . he's bothering you?"

"Worse than that! Why, if I was only bigger—"

"Are you leaving on your own, you big, ugly mollymawk," Lyncher X growled, waddling closer, "or do the guys and I have to—"

75

Angus, suddenly realizing that he *was* bigger, abruptly stiffened and turned. "Aura Lei says you're bothering her."

"So what's that to you, gull-face?" Lyncher X's Sooty friends cackled with glee at their pal's brave humor. "Now get out of here, and leave me alone with the whimpering, whining little chick. Looks like I'm going to have to teach her a little about what's what."

Cocking his head to one side like he had once learned from Aura Lei, Angus rose to his full height and looked down on the lesser Sooty. "Gull-face? Whimpering, whining little chick? Those are bad names, Lyncher X. Very bad names. It looks to me like you're the one who needs to be taught a thing or two." Angus paused, surprised at his own bravery. And an instant later, when a huge stream of foul-smelling oil issued from his bill to cover Lyncher X's neck and chest, he was even more surprised.

"Oh, yuk!" the belligerent Sooty wailed as he looked down. "And I just finished preening!"

"Well, you're going to need to do it again," Angus declared disdainfully, feeling braver by the moment. "But not here!"

"Oh, yeah? And who is going to make me go?"

Puffing his feathers to make himself look even larger, Angus suddenly stepped forward and lashed out with his bill, catching the belligerent Sooty off guard. With a yelp Lyncher X was sent tumbling into the sand, and when he bobbed up, still defiant, he was sent tumbling once again.

76

Then, before the startled gaze of Lyncher X's buddies, Angus waddled over and stared down at the suddenly fearful, groveling bird. "Who's going to make you go? I am," he stated flatly, doing his best to hide the last vestiges of trembling he was still feeling in his legs. "And as long as it's a great distance off, I don't much care where you go. But do it. Now!"

With almost a whimper, and with sudden fear in his eyes, the bully Lyncher X dragged himself to his feet, lumbered off down the beach, and was airborne. "Come on, you guys," he called down sullenly as he circled overhead, "let's go someplace where we're appreciated."

The crowd of Sootys shifted awkwardly as they looked from Lyncher X to each other, and then to Angus. And then one after another they dropped their heads, turned, and waddled off in separate directions.

"Hey, what gives?" Lyncher X shouted downward. "A L, Seb C, Eleazor Dimfoddle, the rest of you— we're together, you guys! Remember?"

"Not anymore, you aren't," Angus declared as he looked upward, suddenly feeling very good about himself. "Now, are you leaving, or do I have to come up there after you?"

Lyncher X gulped fearfully, and without another word wheeled and flapped westward toward the horizon.

"Wow," Howie T breathed, obviously in awe, "I didn't know *anybody* could do that to Lyncher X."

"Haven't you got someplace to go?" Angus asked,

turning back to the Sooty who had once been his closest neighbor. "Some cute little chick to meet or something?"

"Huh? Oh, yeah!" the Sooty gulped, backing awkwardly away. "See you around, Gus. Maybe tonight? Okay? Or tomorrow?"

Angus said nothing, only watched, and quickly turning tail, Howie T waddled humbly away after the others.

"Thank you, Angus Austin," Aura Lei declared sweetly, reaching up and clicking his bill again.

"I didn't do much," the big gray albatross replied, his heart suddenly soaring higher than his body ever had. "Besides, I didn't want that bird troubling my albatrix any longer."

78   And Aura Lei was happy to admit that she was.

...they spent their days gliding wingtip to wingtip...

8

For the next three years Angus and Aura Lei were
never far from each other. Of course they were not
mature enough to mate, and they both understood
that. But they filled each other's ears with joy and
laughter and sweet promises for the future, and they
spent their days gliding wingtip to wingtip as they
followed the changing seasons of the southern hemisphere.

Constantly Angus found himself watching Aura
Lei, examining over and over again each of her lovely
attributes. For she was truly a delightful albatrix, with
the same clear eye as his mother, the same sleek body
and long, sweeping wingspan, and even more amazing, the same unique feather coloring that he had. Of

course she wasn't big and awkward like he was, but that was a plus, too, for no one would ever think to call her any of the horrid names he had become so used to enduring. And he felt great peace about that.

But more than anything else, Angus knew that he felt an overwhelming love for his delightful, beautiful companion. Even more amazing was the fact that she seemed to feel the same about him.

"Isn't it beautiful?" Angus questioned through misty eyes early one morning as they stood together on a tiny speck of rock somewhere in the South Atlantic, examining the sunrise. "It reminds me of that morning we stood on the beach with Leena Joy." And it did, too. The dawn was coming up beyond the sea in the east, and pale fingers of light were caressing the edges of the clouds with brilliance, giving them a golden, filigreed appearance that was absolutely breathtaking.

In silence they watched the light brighten until the sun at last tipped out above the sea, turning the dawn golden and the sea a mass of sparkling jewels, this time reminding Angus of the mornings and evenings he had spent alone as a youth, waiting for his mother to return with dinner.

"I have a question for you," he mused thoughtfully.

"And it is?" Aura Lei smiled.

"Do you ever miss the garbage you used to eat?"

Aura Lei gave him a funny look. "Miss it? How could *anyone* miss eating garbage?"

"I . . . I don't know." Angus was suddenly feeling

awfully foolish. "I just sort of wonder . . . I mean, I never had any, but . . . well, never mind. How do you suppose you ended up not getting the Sooty coloring of plumage?"

Aura Lei laughed. "What a silly question, Angus Austin. You know as well as I do that it's because I stopped eating garbage as soon as I left the nest, and have done all in my power since then to purify myself. That's also why I don't miss it."

"But . . . you are looking more and more like a Royal."

"I am becoming a Royal, silly. Just like you."

Sadly Angus shook his head. "You're wrong, Aura Lei. We're Sootys, not Royals, and I don't care how we look."

Suddenly serious, Aura Lei looked upward at her beloved Angus, cocking her head sideways as she did so. "Very well, if you want to believe we're Sootys, then so be it. But let me say one other thing about Royals and Sootys, something I've thought about for a long time. Tell me. How common are Sootys?"

81

Angus chuckled. "We're everywhere. You know that."

"You're right. The Sooty albatross, which is characterized by mottled feathers, short stumpy wings, and a tendency to fly low and fast and dive heedlessly into the garbage of the world for its dinners and its pleasures, is also the most common albatross.

"The Royal albatross, on the other hand, is a glorious sea bird with a wondrous wide wingspan and a sleek body that enables it to fly far and farther than perhaps any other bird. Unfortunately it is also terribly rare. In fact, one hardly ever sees a Royal. Look around us, Angus. Have we seen even one Royal in the whole time we've been together?"

Thoughtfully Angus shook his head. "No, not any true Royals, at least."

"No, we haven't. But here's what I have come to believe is the great and grand secret of our kind—the difference between the two. Long ago, in the very beginning, Royal albatri and Sooty albatri, wing for wing, leg for leg, bone for bone and feather for feather, were exactly the same. Yet where the majority of albatri flew heedlessly fast and low, looking always downward, seeking grossness and constant gratification, a rare few soared far and farther, high and higher, exercising restraint while they looked beyond themselves, searching for further understanding. And therein developed all the difference between them."

Quizzically Angus looked at Aura Lei. "Are you trying to say that you think the only difference between a Royal and a Sooty is what we take into us?"

"In a way, yes. But the issue isn't so much food, I believe, as it is purity. I'm trying very hard to be pure, Angus Austin, and I believe that's why I'm looking more and more Royal."

Stunned by Aura Lei's reasoning, Angus could only stare out to sea.

"Well? What do you think?"

"I think," he responded finally, even sadly, "that the difference is greater than that, a lot greater. Why,

82

Royals are . . . well, they're practically perfect! And while I believe that may fit you, I know very well that it doesn't fit me."

"I think it does," Aura Lei smiled sweetly. "And that's why I love you so much. I've seen how you reach out to others, especially those such as Leena Joy who are in need, and I love you for that. Besides, you've never polluted yourself with the garbage of this world, and you show no desire to. If that doesn't make you Royal, then I don't know what does. Oh, Angus Austin, you can't know how proud of you I feel!"

"Thank you," Angus replied, feeling embarrassed and therefore determined to end the conversation. "But you and I both know the real truth, which is that I crave garbage as much as the next bird. I just haven't had the courage to break the promise I made my mother.

"Now, what say we race each other to that cloud out there."

Later that spring, following an inner cue that neither of them could really explain, Angus and Aura Lei returned to their island colony to look around, for after they mated they would build their nest there. But when they arrived and began waddling about, things got a little ugly. No matter whether Aura Lei was beside him or not, Angus was still Angus Awkward, and he was so big and clumsy that he couldn't help but live the part. Worse, there seemed no end of Sootys to remind him of it.

"Get out of the way," a Sooty warned sarcastically,

83

"or you'll be trampled by Gus the awkward one."

"Here comes Gus, the albatross earthquake," another snickered. And so it went. Mocking, jeers and laughter followed Angus everywhere.

This was made worse by the fact that Aura Lei had been right about his feathers. Once he finished molting and preening in this, the seventh year of his life, Angus found himself looking for all the world like a Royal. And of course the members of his friendly Sooty neighborhood were more than willing to confirm Angus's belief that it was all a sham.

"Look, Mom," a Sooty nestling exclaimed as he waddled past, "it's a Royal, a true Royal."

"Don't you be fooled by plumage," the mother intoned with solemn and dignified air. "That's only Angus Awkward, you know. He and that Aura Lei are both Sootys, they grew up right here with the rest of us, and it's a disgrace how they're trying to be something they're not!"

84

Needless to say, Angus and Aura Lei did not remain long on the island that summer. But they were so in love, and so happy in the presence of each other, that neither felt deeply troubled by the small-minded Sootys.

"I have a question to ask you," Aura Lei stated on another beautiful day nearly a year later, when they had been constant companions for nearly four years. That day they were moving southward, off the eastern coast of Australia, and the schools of squid had been so plentiful that they had hardly traveled at all in the past several weeks.

"And your question is?" Angus asked, feeling as if he could never eat again in his whole mortal life, he was so full.

"Well, actually, I have two questions. First, what do you think your mother used to mean when she told you to fly far and farther and high and higher, seeking understanding beyond the far and distant horizon?"

"I don't know," Angus replied thoughtfully. "She never would explain it. But the big Royal told me the same thing, you know."

"He did?"

"Uh-huh. And it still doesn't make any sense."

"I'm bothered by it, too." Aura Lei looked troubled. "After all, we've done nothing but fly far and farther, high and higher, every day for the past four years. And beyond every far and distant horizon is merely another one. Is that the understanding you were supposed to seek?"

85

Angus grinned. "I don't think so. But if it is, then as long as I can keep seeking it with you, I'll be happy forever."

Aura Lei beamed. "What a dear, sweet thing to say! Thank you, Angus Austin. But . . . uh . . . I'm afraid that won't be possible."

Stunned, Angus glanced at the lovely albatrix who he had always believed would one day be his mate. "What? But I thought . . . I thought—"

Aura Lei laughed delightedly. "What I mean, honey," she explained, cocking her head to the side and looking up at him slyly, "is that it's almost time for us to return to the colony and establish a nest to-gether."

"You mean . . . you mean—"

"I mean," and Aura Lei blushed slightly when she said it, "and this is my second question; I feel it is time for us to become mates. Will you have me?"

"Will I have you?" Angus blurted. "Omasquawk, Aura Lei, of course I'll have you! Forever! And you . . . you'll really have me?"

"I have never wanted anyone else, my darling."

If Angus thought he had been happy before, then once he and Aura Lei had made their eternal vows—for as everyone knows, albatri never mate for less than forever—he *knew* he was happy. Aura Lei became more beautiful to him, the sky and the sea became more incredible and enticing than they had ever been, the squid they found together tasted better than ever, and . . . well, for Angus, everything was simply BETTER than it had ever been in his life!

And that happiness was compounded one day in October of their ninth year of life, when winter had finally broken and the green of spring was on the earth, for on that day Aura Lei casually informed Angus that they needed to get moving if they intended to establish a nest on the island in time.

"Omasquawk! Omasquawk!" Angus kept repeating, too stunned to squawk anything else. "We'd better hurry, Aura Lei! We'd better . . . omasquawk! Can you fly? I mean, will it hurt the egg?"

Aura Lei laughed delightedly. "I didn't say I had

an egg growing within me, Angus. I merely said it was time to get started toward our island so we could establish a nest."

"So . . . so there isn't an egg?" Angus Austin was definitely disappointed.

"I don't think so." Aura Lei beamed at the love she could see in Angus's face. "But one day soon there will be an egg, I'm sure of it. That's why we really should be moving toward our island."

And so they did, day after day, as Angus did all he could to take care of his beloved mate. And day after day he grew more in love with her, and more excited about the prospect of becoming the father of his own little hatchling.

But then, when he least expected such a thing to happen, Angus felt a strange, sudden urge to preen his molting feathers. Surprisingly, he was alone, for Aura Lei was behind him, coming more slowly while he hurried ahead hunting food. Glancing down he saw that he was over a small speck of land south of New Zealand, so with a twinge of guilt that he was momentarily abandoning his errand he banked, glided down, and landed on the rocky shore.

He had not expected the place to be inhabited, had not even thought that it might be. But he hadn't been preening long before he realized that he had inadvertently touched down near a tiny colony of Royal albatri—four nests, to be exact.

For what seemed a long time Angus stood preening, watching the Royals all the while but trying not to

87

appear too obvious. He had seen only the one Royal in all his life, and the thought of four nesting pairs of them was almost more than he could imagine. Maybe, he thought with some excitement, one of them would be the bird who had saved both his and his mother's lives. But as he lingered, that particular Royal did not appear. In fact, only one Royal, a female, came out of the sky while Angus watched, and her appearance generated so much excitement among the others that Angus began to wonder if something might be amiss.

For a moment the Royal albatrix looked down at her mate, the only male present, who was obviously keeping their egg warm. Then, after they had clicked bills once or twice, she waddled to one of the other nests and began regurgitating food for the nesting fe-

male. Angus watched in amazement as the single albatrix fed first one and then another of the nesting albatri, leaving her mate until last. Then, after he had refused to grope the last vestiges of food from her gullet, she took his place and he lifted off into the darkening sky.

Because Aura Lei had not as yet caught up with him Angus continued to wait, pondering the situation and feeling worse with each passing moment. Almost certainly something had happened to the three missing albatri, something that was preventing them from sharing incubation duties with their mates. Worse, the situation had obviously left the food-gathering responsibilities for four individuals upon the shoulders of one—a difficult task that would become impossible with the hatching of the eggs.

Angus knew he should volunteer his services, but he absolutely did not want to do so. By staying and helping he would eliminate his and Aura Lei's chances of having a chick this season. And there was nothing he could think of that would be more important than that. So he must not stay! He must not.

Several times Angus lifted his wings in preparation for a running start and takeoff from the beach. But each time he made the mistake of first glancing at the nesting Royals, and knowing their need, he just couldn't do it. He also thought constantly about the Royal who had come to save him and his mother, and though he hadn't much liked what the gleaming white bird had done to him, he was very grateful for the Royal's gift of life.

Still, Aura Lei would be along any minute, and—

"Sir? Are you the Chosen One sent to help us?"

Startled from his reverie, Angus spun about to face the Royal albatrix who had come up behind him. "Huh?" he responded lamely.

"We do not know what has happened to our mates, but we have been praying that someone would be chosen to assist us in keeping our nestlings alive. Are you that Chosen One?"

Slowly Angus shook his head, thinking as he did so that Leena Joy had shared the same foolish notion. "I just stopped to preen, ma'am. I haven't been chosen for anything."

"Oh. I see." The simple, yet painful, acceptance cut Angus to the heart. But so did the thoughts of Aura Lei nesting alone on the distant island, just as these birds were doing. Still—

"I suppose because you are a Royal, we thought you would be the Chosen One."

Angus chuckled. "I'm not a Royal, ma'am."

Her eyes wide with surprise, the albatrix examined him carefully. "You're not?"

"Not hardly! I'm just a big, awkward, ugly gray Sooty."

"Imagine that," the Royal mother said softly. And then, without another squawk, she turned and waddled back toward her earthen nest.

Feeling worse than he had ever felt—so torn inside that he could hardly stand it—Angus took a single hesitant step after the sorrowing mother. "Uh . . . ma'am? Could I ask a question?"

90

"Of course," she replied, pausing and turning back.

"Have any of the nestlings hatched out?"

"Two," she replied sadly. "Yesterday. Mine should hatch out in about two weeks, and the other not for a week or two after that. It is why we are so concerned—why we pleaded with the Creator that one be chosen and sent to help us. I . . . I am sorry it isn't you." And with that she turned and continued to waddle away.

"Well, it isn't me!" Angus squawked after her. "As soon as my mate arrives, we'll be on our way to build a nest of our own. And she's the only one who has chosen me!"

"We understand," the Royal mother called back over her gleaming shoulder. "Go with joy."

"I will," Angus grumbled to himself as he took

three or four lumbering steps toward takeoff. "I mean, who do you think you are, making me feel guilty."

"It's a real problem, Aura Lei," Angus explained as he and his mate circled above the tiny island several hours later. "And I feel so torn that I can hardly stand it!"

Aura Lei was very quiet. "What do you think you should do?" she finally asked.

"I should be with you! I mean, I *have* to be if we're going to have an egg together."

"And I want you with me," Aura Lei said as tears of sorrow dropped from her eyes. "But Angus Austin, darling—"

"I know," Angus said, his own heart heavy with foreboding. "I know! I can't just leave and allow the Royals down there to perish. If I did that, I could never live with myself. But Aura Lei, if it takes too long to care for them—if their Chosen One doesn't come—then I don't know what I'll do."

91

Aura Lei smiled through her tears. "Angus, darling, everything will work out. If we miss this season, then there is always another. But that won't happen, I know it won't. You'll come in time. Besides, this is the right thing for you to do, and we both know the Creator always takes care of those who do right.

"Oh, my darling, I can't tell you how proud of you I feel! Even if you aren't a Royal, you're the most Royal-acting bird I've ever known!"

"I'll be there, Aura Lei," Angus called as his mate turned alone toward the distant colony. "I promise you, I'll come!"

"I know," Aura Lei called back, her voice already distant. "And I promise you I'll be waiting."

She said something more, but her words were lost in the distance. And then Aura Lei was gone, leaving Angus truly alone for the first time in four long and wonderful years. And so with a sigh that was more a shudder of fear, Angus dropped his wing and turned back toward the tiny, troubled colony of Royals.

"I . . . I guess I'll help until your Chosen One comes," he called down as he approached. "But only until then!"

"Thank you, O Chosen One," they all called up.

"Oh for crying out loud . . ." Angus grumbled with disgust, then called, "I'll be back as soon as possible with some food."

92

"Remember, we only eat—"

"I know, I know, I know," Angus shouted downward with resignation. "You only eat squid. Don't worry. Even if it takes longer to find, that's what I'll get. And let's hope that Chosen One of yours is here by the time I get back. Because I'll be gone then, I promise you! I can't keep my Aura Lei waiting any longer."

And with a strange stab of pure joy that he was again helping someone piercing the sorrow and pain he felt, Angus scuttled eastward before the wind, preparing to enter into the ellipses that had become so much a part of his heretofore wonderful life.

"Why du I luuk so bad?" Lyncher X growled weakly. "Because I can't find anything to eat, you big, dumb bird."

9

For six weeks Angus assisted the struggling colony of Royals, bringing them the finest squid he could find from as far away as he had to go. And though he asked the Royals several times to call him Gus, he even grew used to being called their Chosen One. In his heart he understood how ridiculous the idea was, but he finally concluded that their delusion was harmless, and it was far easier to ignore it than to constantly argue it down.

Still, Angus was not the best of help to the Royals. Oh, he brought their squid regularly, and he spoke when spoken to. But his patience was always short, and he lost no opportunity to let them know that he needed to be on his way as quickly as possible—or sooner. For his beloved Aura Lei was waiting, he reminded them again and again, and he needed to be with her.

And truly, Angus never stopped thinking of Aura Lei and worrying about her. But then one day as he was flying ellipses and thinking of what a great sacrifice he was making, he found himself wondering, for the first time ever, about his own Royal Chosen One. What had that great bird sacrificed? What had he been forced to miss out on? During the weeks and weeks that he did nothing but seek out squid for Angus and his mother, what personal things had he set aside?

Try as he would, Angus could not remember any sign that the Royal had been distressed, or that he had felt irritated at not being elsewhere. Yet somewhere he must have had a nest of his own, and a mate who was as Royal as himself.

Such considerations startled Angus, who added things together in the middle of his ellipse and came to the inescapable conclusion that his own service to the Royals left a great deal to be desired. Even though he was not Royal, and even though he was not their Chosen One, it had been his choice to help, not theirs. Therefore, he determined a little guiltily, he had better start smiling more and being more tender and compassionate. He had better stop trying to make the helpless Royals pay for his inconvenience. In short, Angus concluded, he had better start acting more like his own Royal Chosen One had acted. He owed the great bird that much, at least!

94

So he changed, very quickly, and the helpless Royal mothers were more than astounded. At first they disbelieved, but then they began to reciprocate Angus's new warmth, and in a very short time Angus found that he had grown absolutely fond of them all.

Thus, when the Royal mothers were at last able to leave their nestlings to search the seas for their own squid, Angus found himself incapable of saying good-by. He was filled with too many emotions, and too much love. And besides, he had every intention of keeping track of the mothers and their little nestlings just as the old Royal had kept track of him. So one morning before dawn he slipped quietly away, and in doing so, he at last understood, at least partially, why his own Royal benefactor had left without saying good-by.

With a strange sense of sorrow and loneliness Angus pushed eastward, giving thanks to the Creator as he flew that he had been allowed to help the Royals. But he also felt true freedom, and so he gave thanks as well that he would finally be able to join his beloved mate, and get about the business of creating an egg and bringing a little hatchling into the world.

For an entire day Angus made wonderful time, which made him hopeful of reaching Aura Lei within the week. But then, when he least expected such an encounter, Angus ran into his old nemesis, Lyncher X.

"Gus," the bedraggled bird gasped as he struggled pitifully along beneath a mackerel sky of cirrocumulus clouds, "am I glad to see you!"

"Hello, Lynch." Angus was not pleased, for he had

been climbing to catch the high winds he knew were above the clouds, rippling them into their fish-scale appearance. Running into Lyncher X was not only threatening to him, but would surely hinder him from hurrying to Aura Lei. "You . . . uh . . . you don't look so good," he added lamely.

Lyncher X grinned ruefully. "And that isn't anything to how I feel."

Angus could believe that, for the Sooty did not look well at all. His eyes were sunken and hollow, his bill was a pasty color, his feathers were splotchy and thin, and he truly looked like he was wasting away.

"What're you doing way out here?"

"That's what I'd like to know!" The Sooty shook his head in disgust. "I thought maybe I could find a fishing trawler to follow, but I haven't seen one in days—maybe weeks. If I don't find one soon, Gus, I . . . I think I'm going to starve to death!"

"But . . . why?" Angus was dumbfounded.

"Why?" Lyncher X growled weakly. "Because I can't find anything to eat, you big, dumb bird."

Angus shook his head in amazement. "What happened to the trawler you were following with the flock?"

"The flock drove me out, in case you hadn't heard."

"I hadn't." Angus almost smiled, but managed to control himself. "I heard there was another flock a day or two north," he said then, trying to be both tactful and helpful.

Lyncher X nodded. "There is. They drove me out a year ago. Over the years, so have three or four others.

I . . . I'm a failure, Gus—an absolute failure! Nobody wants me for a mate, nobody even wants me around! Tell the truth, I think maybe you're the only bird in the whole world who'll even talk to me, and I wouldn't blame you if you didn't."

Lyncher X's emaciated body was racked with a series of coughs, and watching him, Angus had absolutely no idea what to do. Besides, he had made Aura Lei a promise.

"Go on and go," Lyncher X gasped as his coughing subsided, speaking as if he had read Angus's thoughts. "You've got things to do, Gus, and I'm a goner anyway."

"Hey," Angus grumbled with a feeling of terrible resignation, for once again he knew that he couldn't leave this desperate bird to perish, "don't worry about me. I'll be fine. But let me ask you a question, Lynch. Why aren't you getting something to eat right now? What are you doing flying so high?"

Lyncher X looked at Angus as if the big bird was crazy. "Because if I get much lower, you big lummox, I'll splash. Besides, you see any trawlers down there, chucking out offal for me to dine on?"

Angus laughed. "No. But there's food other than offal, Lynch. Hasn't anybody ever taught you how to fly an ellipse?"

"A how much?"

"An ellipse. It's what you fly when you're hunting for the best food an albatross ever ate. Come on, and I'll show you how it's done."

"I'm warning you, Gus," Lyncher X said, a look of

desperate fear in his sunken eyes. "If I go much lower, I'm in the water! And I don't think I have the strength to get back out again."

Again Angus laughed. "A little seawater won't hurt you. Fact is, it might even help. Now, the first thing to do is turn your tail into the wind and make a run with it, building up speed. Follow me, and I'll show you. . . . No, keep your tail straight, more aligned with your body. That's good, Lynch! Almost perfect! Now, stretch your wings out—further, further."

And so over the course of the next several days Angus taught Lyncher X the basic points of flying the ellipse. And though the Sooty splashed dozens and dozens of times, Angus was always able to talk him into the air again, until gradually he got the hang of it. More amazingly, twice during the course of instruction they passed over huge schools of squid, which after some difficulty Angus talked Lyncher X into at least trying.

Fortunately the famished bird was hungry enough to eat almost anything, besides which for his entire life he had been eating almost anything anyway. So it didn't take him long to appreciate the fine taste and excellent rubbery texture of the squid. In fact, after two very satisfying meals he declared with certainty that in his opinion, the tentacled tidbit was the finest food on the face of the planet.

"So that's really all there is to it?" he asked a few days later as he completed a very successful ellipse. "That's how an albatross is supposed to hunt for his food?"

98

Angus smiled. "It's how the Royal taught me."

"Aha! So this is the Royal way," Lyncher X declared thoughtfully. "Well, it's easier than constantly fighting the flock, it's nowhere near as hard on the old body, it's quiet and peaceful out here, and the taste of the main course is superb. No wonder you Royals keep it to yourselves."

"Hey, Lynch."

The Sooty chuckled. "Just kidding, Gus. If you don't want to say you're a Royal, that's fine by me. Tell the truth, though, I can't imagine why every bird in the world doesn't do ellipses and eat squid."

"You . . . you'd really rather eat this than garbage?"

Lyncher eyed Angus narrowly. "Are you crazy? I'd rather eat squid every day of the week and ten times on Sunday! Why do you ask?"

"Oh," Angus responded, feeling as foolish as he'd felt questioning Aura Lei, "sometimes I sort of wonder what I maybe missed."

"Well," Lyncher X said with a harsh laugh, "you missed being called lots of degrading names; you missed being practically beaten to death by frenzied, selfish birds; you missed the awful taste of offal; you missed the horrid stench of it that permeates your body from one sun to the next; you missed polluting yourself and turning your feathers all Sooty; and there's probably a lot more similar stuff you've missed that I can't even think of. If I were you, Gus, I'd count your blessings that your mom turned you into a Royal."

99

"She didn't, Lynch," Angus sighed. "She just made me look like one."

With a shake of his head to show that he disagreed, Lyncher X grinned. "Whatever you say, Gus. Whatever you say."

"Well," Angus responded quietly as his eyes lifted to the far and distant horizon. "It's been fun, Lynch. But I've got a mate to go find."

"Say," the Sooty interrupted, "I've been meaning to tell you that I saw Aura Lei in the colony."

"Was . . . was she all right?"

"I think so, but she wouldn't squawk with me."

"Gotta go!" Angus screeched as he lifted into the air. "Good luck, Lynch!"

"You too, Gus. And thanks!"

100　And with the wind whistling through his primaries, Angus strained his rejuvenated muscles and sped onward toward the tiny island so many days and lifetimes away.

Angus was late,
he realized
with sorrow, for
Aura Lei was gone.

10

Tragically for Angus, it was not until the second day of May that he finally got to the island. A heavy winter snow, driven by the bitterly cold wind, was beating against the rocks and filling the empty nests where the colony had raised their young. With an empty feeling in the pit of his stomach Angus looked around, but it only took a moment to see that the island had been abandoned. There were not even prints in the newly fallen snow. Angus was too late, he realized with sorrow, for Aura Lei was gone.

"Why?" he shrieked at the Creator as he lifted his face to the snow-shrouded sky. "Why have you let this happen? All I ever wanted was to be with Aura Lei and to have my own nestling. Was that too much to expect? Couldn't someone else have helped all your . . . your charity cases?"

With tears of sorrow and frustration, Angus waddled aimlessly along the beach. And the others *had* been charity cases, too, one after another. First it had been the Royals, then Lyncher X, then that wounded albatrix who hadn't been able to find her daughters, and then two weeks with those young Sootys who had been foolish enough to get frozen in the ice at the mouth of that river, and finally that old Laysan albatross who had been dying, and had pleaded with Angus to stay with him.

"You see what I mean?" Angus said, his voice breaking with sorrow. "I'm such a sucker that I can't say no to anybody—anybody, that is, but my dear, sweet Aura Lei. O Great Creator, please watch over her, and help me to find her."

In despair he lifted into the wind, and day after day he drifted aimlessly, riding the hurricane-force Polar Easterlies westward, then getting turned around by a massive storm system and carried back to the east on the churning Southern Westerlies. His wanderings were made even more aimless by the fact that that particular winter was one of the worst the southern hemisphere had ever known. Storm after storm buffeted both the South Pacific and the South Atlantic. Angus was battered and buffeted with them, and was forced to expend so much of his energy beating his wings against the furious wind currents that he also had to spend too much time flying ellipses down low and searching for food.

102

But in the days that followed his discovery of the abandoned colony, Angus did his best to continue searching. High or low, fast or slow, his round, round eyes were relentless in their probing of the nooks and crannies of every coastline, every island, and even every speck of rocky upthrust that he happened to find. And over and over, whenever he fell in with fellow birds, he asked the same question: Had they seen a beautiful Sooty albatrix who looked like a Royal and who was called by the name Aura Lei?

Only, no bird had seen her, and over time Angus very nearly gave up in despair. In fact, his spirits drooped lower and lower until he was no longer certain that he even wanted to live. There was no joy in his life, no hope in his heart. Nothing mattered any longer, nothing.

103

Without intending to, Angus had turned and was moving north, where the air was warmer and winter hardly thought of. And there, on a dark and gloomy day when he was at the very rock-bottom of his life, he saw below him a flock of birds following a fishing trawler.

For some time he only watched them, aware of their wheeling and diving into the offal but paying little attention to it. And then, gradually, he began to consider the joy they seemed to be finding in their search for garbage. Over and over their distant cries reached his ears, and it seemed to Angus that he could even distinguish between the squawks of joy when they splashed into the best of the worst, and the shrieks of frustration when they missed.

Maybe, he thought with a heavy sigh, he could find a little solace in garbage. After all, Sootys everywhere, and gulls, petrels, and shearwaters, too, sought after it all their natural lives. They seemed to be happy, too, which was all he had ever wanted to be. And maybe he would be fortunate enough to splash into the very best of the worst.

But wait a minute! Wait just a squid-plucking minute! Blinking a little reality into his eyes, Angus took a deep breath. That was *garbage* down there, he reminded himself—rotten, awful offal! And he wasn't going to start polluting himself with it just because he was lonely.

More significantly, he had made his mother a promise which he had never broken. That promise had always been sacred to him, and that integrity was one of the things Aura Lei had told him she cherished most in her mate. What would she think, when they got together again—and Angus suddenly knew they *would* get together again—if she found he was no longer a bird of his word?

No sir! he resolved with a strong upward push of his wings. Even if he never saw Aura Lei again in this life he was not going to break his promise! No matter how miserable he was, no matter how lonely, he would remain true to himself, true to those he loved!

"O Great Creator," he breathed as he wheeled back toward the wintery south where he was sure he would find Aura Lei, "thank you for helping me to avoid that mistake. I . . . I'm not really sure why I have been so tempted, but I'm glad you helped me re-member who I am supposed to be.

"Now, if I could only have a little help in finding my beloved."

Another week passed, and then most of another, and the only thing that changed for Angus was that he was back in the region of storms again. "You see, O Great Creator?" he said one day as he was skitter-ing along at about a thousand feet, sitting practically on the front teeth of a howling blizzard that was mostly behind and below him, "these storms are keeping me from finding my Aura Lei. I'm sure of it! Of course I'm thankful for that fine meal of squid you brought me a few hours ago, but now I'm too heavy to do any real searching. I know I allowed the wind to carry me too high to see anything down below, but if I work my way any lower the snow will blind me and I won't be able to see anything anyway. You see the dilemma?"

105

All around the hapless bird the huge cumulonim-bus clouds billowed and boiled, high and higher, with fierce winds and pelting rain, hail and snow car-ried about on the updrafts and downdrafts of the dreaded thunderheads, until it seemed to Angus as if he had become an insignificant speck in the endless immensity of creation.

"I . . . I guess I'm not much for you to pay attention to," he whispered as he subconsciously lifted his right wing to balance against a sudden gust of wind, "and I'm truly sorry I haven't been flying far and farther, high and higher, keeping my eye on the distant horizon where I might discover understanding. I know those things are important, O Great One, and I absolutely intend to do them. But I would like to find Aura Lei first. If you could help even a little, well, I'd appreciate it more than I can say. Once she is by my side again, I promise I will get back to the business of trying to find understanding."

Angus was given no chance to continue, for a furious microburst of wind suddenly slashed down from the sky, catching him and sending him reeling out of control toward the sea.

With a mighty screech of fear and shock Angus fought back, straining with all his soul to right himself and hold his wings where they could carry him rather than pull him downward into a splash. But no matter what he tried, no matter how he strained to right himself and pull from his tailspin, he could gain no control. He was going to splash.

It wasn't that Angus feared the water, for he was a very good paddler. It was just that he knew he was back in the general area of his island, and so he also knew that there were rocks jutting out everywhere below him. At the speed he was being pushed downward, even if he slammed into just water the impact could seriously damage his aviatic career. And if he slammed into the rocks? Well, Angus didn't want to think about that, not at all. What he wanted was to find his beloved Aura Lei.

Finally, when only a few yards separated him from the churning and lashing waves, Angus managed to pull out of his horrific tailspin. Stretching his wings to as near their ten-and-a-half-foot length as he could, and thrusting his big feet forward as airbrakes, Angus flashed before the wind at a dizzying speed. He knew he was going at least a hundred miles an hour and probably a great deal faster; the water and rocks below and around him were little more than a blur, and the sleet was burning his eyes and clogging his tubular nostrils so that he could neither see nor breathe.

Somehow he had to slow down, either that or climb against the furious wind pressure that was pushing down on him. Angus was too low for some of the rocks and small islands that dotted the area, and he could slam head-on into one of them without either seeing it or having time to avoid it. Yet even with his high-lift secondaries straining to the utmost, he was gaining no altitude, nor slowing even a notch. It was almost as if—

And then abruptly the wind eased and the microburst veered away. And Angus, straining so hard to both slow and climb, suddenly found himself lifted into a perfect overhead loop, something he had never even imagined possible. As he plummeted downward out of the loop, straining again to level out before he splashed, a tiny sheltered cove between some huge rocks flashed past his view—a place where he might plop into the water and at least catch his breath before continuing his endless search.

Letting his airspeed carry him up and around in a tight arc that wasn't quite another loop, Angus dropped his left wing, slipped the wind, slid between

107

two upthrusts of the dark, wet stone, and settled easily into the tiny area of almost calm water.

Closing his eyes he breathed deeply, settling his nerves. Then, knowing he should probably ride out the storm in this place, Angus lifted his heavy eyelids to look about—and discovered instantly that he was not alone.

"H . . . hello," he said, and his greeting was almost more a gasp of surprise than a proper hello. "I . . . I didn't know I had company."

The other bird, obviously terrified, said nothing, and as Angus looked more closely, he could see that he was sharing the tiny cove with a young albatrix. "Are you all right?" he asked kindly, pushing from his mind the thought that here was another bird he would have to help, another charity case thrown mercilessly at him.

108

"I . . . I'm afraid," the albatrix stammered through her chattering bill.

Angus smiled as reassuringly as he could. "I don't blame you. But you picked a nice spot here—good shelter from the wind, wonderful protection from the biggest waves. That was smart thinking."

"I got blown in here," the albatrix stated simply. "I didn't pick anything. Are you another of the Chosen Ones?"

"Not hardly." Angus chuckled, wondering where that silly phrase had ever started. "Some other birds called me that once, a long time ago. But they were as wrong as you are."

"You're here, aren't you?" she asked innocently.

"Well, yes," Angus was forced to admit, "I am here. But I'm definitely not chosen."

The albatrix looked terribly disappointed. "When my mother asked the Creator for help when I was only a chick," she declared, "He sent a Chosen One. I've been asking for help for days, and so I thought . . . I thought—" And the frightened young bird closed her round, round eyes and began to weep.

"Hey," Angus pleaded, his big heart once again swelling with compassion, "if that's a `sorrow' cry, or a `feel sorry for myself' cry, then there's no need for it. If all you need is help, then chosen or not, I'm the bird for you. I'll do whatever I can. That means a `happy' cry is legitimate, so if that's what your tears are for, then go ahead and enjoy them."

Through her tears the albatrix smiled sheepishly, and from that moment she began to relax. Not that she and Angus talked a lot, of course, for the roar of the storm made that difficult. Besides, the albatrix didn't seem inclined to talk, and the last thing Angus wanted to do was to get too deeply involved with another bird. He didn't want to know her name; he wasn't about to tell her his; and life histories were strictly out.

Of course, he couldn't just leave her stranded, either. So there had to be at least a minimal amount of conversation.

"Was it the storm that frightened you?" Angus asked a little later.

"Y . . . yes."

"Then we'll wait it out together. Afterward, I'll tell

you how to get to where it's warmer."

"But . . . I can't fly!" And again the albatrix dissolved into tears.

"You can't fly?" Angus was instantly more concerned. "Are you hurt?"

"N . . . no. I just . . . don't know how!"

"And how do you know that?" Angus asked, suppressing a slight smile.

"Because when my mother didn't come back for a very long time, I tried. I did just what she told me, too. Only . . . only I went down like a rock! Splash! And then this storm came, and I've been in the water ever since."

"And you're worried that you might drown?"

"Not exactly." The young albatrix sniffled back more tears. "I . . . I'm more afraid of fish—big ones! Mom saw a Sooty get snapped right off the water once, just like that! Ever since she told me about it I've had these horrible dreams. Now I keep thinking I feel something touching my feet."

"Sometimes seaweed can feel scary," Angus agreed. "That's because it's all slimy and gooey, and the currents of water make it move like it's alive. But this is pretty shallow water in this cove, so I'd say we're safe. Why on earth did your mother ever tell you such an awful story?"

The albatrix was embarrassed. "She was trying to keep me from swimming out to join a flock of Sootys that were following a trawler."

"You wanted to join a flock even before you could

fly?"

"Well," she smiled shyly, "she knew I was lonely and hungry, and . . . and I guess I was always sort of a rebel, too. Tell the truth, I think I wanted to swim out there mostly because she said I shouldn't—her and that big, dumb Royal she called the Chosen One.

"Oh," and the embarrassment was suddenly back in the albatrix's demeanor, "I'm sorry! I didn't mean to say bad things about Royals, you being one and all."

Angus chuckled. "I'm not a Royal. I just happen to have Royal plumage. And I've been told so many times how big and dumb and awkward I am that it doesn't even matter anymore. Besides, when I was a nestling I had a big, dumb Royal in my life, too."

"You did?"

111

"I'll say!" Angus was already regretting his loquaciousness, but the young bird was waiting for him to continue, and he could see no polite alternative—nothing except changing the subject as quickly as possible. "He hardly ever said a word," Angus continued, "but time after time he brought me squid to eat, and—oh, my goodness, I completely forgot to ask. Have you had anything to eat lately?"

Soberly the young albatrix shook her head.

"I ate a whole school of squid just before this storm hit. In fact, that's probably why I got smashed around so much by the wind. I was just too heavy. Anyway, get a little closer, and I'll share as much of it with you as you'd like."

"You . . . you would do that for me?"

"Nothing would give me greater pleasure," Angus declared, again pushing thoughts of his missing sweetheart from his mind. "Now here," he said as he opened wide his bill. "Dig innh, ahhnd ehnjohhy."

And with a sob of relief and gratitude, the young albatrix did just that.

112

...Angus was soon hovering directly above
the astonished young albatrix...

11

"Hold your wings out," Angus said the next morning
when it seemed that the storm was lessening. "I'd like
to look at your secondaries."

"Why?" the young albatrix asked, still not quite certain about this big bird who only looked like a Royal.

Angus was patient. "Because the more I look at
you, the more it seems like your feathers are mature
enough to support you in flight. I've got to be on my
way, but I don't feel good about leaving you here in
the water, and I can't just stay here with you the rest
of the winter, either."

Obediently the albatrix stretched out first her left
wing and then her right, allowing Angus to probe her
feathers with his bill.

"Well?" she asked when he had finished, "what do you think?"

"I think," Angus said, "that I'd like to know your name."

"What does that have to do with my feathers?"

"Nothing." Angus smiled, hoping to relax both himself and the albatrix. "But if we're going to be spending a little time together, it would be nice knowing what to call you."

The albatrix smiled. "Okay. My name's Alisha Dee. What's yours?"

"Mine is . . . well, some birds call me Gus, and that will do just fine. Alisha Dee, I'm positive your plumage is mature enough to sustain flight." Angus took a deep breath, at the same time pushing aside his concerns for his missing mate. Obviously the Creator had decided against his finding her, and if he was going to keep from going crazy, he had to accept that and get on with whatever was left of the shambles of his life. "Would you like to learn to fly?" he finally concluded.

114

Slowly, and very fearfully, the albatrix nodded.

"Good." Angus smiled widely. "Now, the main thing is not to be afraid. The Creator designed our wings to give maximum lift with minimum effort. In other words, most of the time we only have to hold them in an extended position and we stay in the air."

"Serious?" Alisha Dee was astonished. "Then why did I fall?"

"Any number of reasons, all of which we'll pro-bably cover later on. But remember, always face into the wind during takeoff. Also, hold your wings as far out as possible. And finally, when you feel the wind lifting you, relax and let it do the work. You ready to give it a try?"

"Could you show me, Gus? Please?"

Angus smiled. "Of course!" And carefully he paddled out of the safety of the tiny cove. "The wind's better out here," he called back to the wide-eyed Alisha Dee. "Now, watch carefully." And facing into the wind and extending his wings, Angus was lifted effortlessly from the water.

Turning slightly cross-wind and allowing the wind to carry him backward, he was soon hovering directly above the astonished albatrix.

"See? Not much to it, if you let the wind do all the work." He smiled again. "Now, paddle out a few yards past that point, hold your wings ready to extend, wait for a wave to lift you into the wind, and you'll be up."

115

"I . . . I'm afraid," Alisha Dee responded, and for the first time Angus noted that the albatrix's body was trembling.

"That's understandable," he soothed as he maintained his position with subconscious movements of his primaries and secondaries. "Any bird in your position would be. But if you'll remember that you were designed by the Creator to be the perfect flyer, it should make things a little less frightening. Now, go ahead, and let's see you fly."

With a brave little smile Alisha Dee did as Angus had instructed, and a moment or so later she, too, was lifted into the air. For an instant she was exhilarated. But when she realized that the powerful wind was carrying her both backward and upward quite rapidly, she shrieked, instinctively tucked her wings, and in the next instant she splashed. Hard. And deep.

"Oh, yes," Angus said as she came sputtering to the surface, "I forgot to tell you. Whatever you do, don't panic and tuck your wings! Once you have them extended, you must lock them in place and keep them there."

"But . . . but I was going *backwards!*" The albatrix was still trying to get the seawater out of her eyes.

Plopping back down into the churning waves, Angus paddled to her side. "I know. So did I. Remember?"

"But . . . how do I go forward?"

Angus grinned. "By turning around and going the other way."

Of course he was teasing, but the young, dripping albatrix was in no mood for humor. "Very funny, Gus. Now what am I really supposed to do?"

"Actually," Angus said, wiping the grin from his face, "about what I said. Turn with the wind. Remember, the object of the type of flying we do is to let the air do most of the work. If the air is calm it won't support you, so you have to move it beneath yourself by flapping your wings. But if the air is moving by itself, which of course is called wind, then all you have to do is make sure that enough of it blows under your wings to support you. Do that, and *voila*, you are flying. Do you understand?"

"I . . . uh . . . I guess so."

Angus was dubious. "Well, you'll see what I mean once we're up there. But remember, the Creator designed the wing of an albatross for maximum lift. That's why you can get airborne off the top of a wave if you have a little breeze that you can face into. When the wind is really howling, however, you can only face it briefly or you'll shoot straight into the air, higher and higher, until the air gets so thin you can no longer breathe. To prevent that, once you get airborne you quickly turn with the wind, which stops your climb."

"So . . . I just let the wind blow me where it wants?" Alisha Dee was skeptical, and it showed.

"You can," Angus agreed, "but you travel pretty fast that way, and I wouldn't recommend it until you've developed better control."

The albatrix shook her head. "Wait a minute! If I can't face the wind because it'll make me climb, and I can't face away from it because it'll make me go too fast, what am I supposed to do?"

"Glide across it," Angus declared simply. "In a high wind, and most often even in a slow one, that's the best way you have of controlling both your altitude and your speed. More importantly, by tacking back and forth, going across the wind first one way and then another, you can actually control your direction. And if you head obliquely into it and then tack back and forth, you can make amazing headway against it.

"Come on. Let's get into the air again, and I'll show you."

117

Quickly Angus lifted off, and with a deep breath Alisha Dee did the same. "Now don't tuck those wings!" Angus shouted as they rose a very fast hundred feet into the air. "Good! Now roll a little onto your side . . . no, lift your right wing higher. . . . Yes! That's good. Now level out, good, good . . . wonderful! Okay, now you're flying!"

"I . . . I am?"

"Of course you are!" Angus smiled with pride. "And you're doing it very well. Let's glide for awhile, okay? And let you get the feel of it."

"Don't I . . . have to flap?"

"Not in the wind," Angus laughed. "Remember, Alisha Dee, the wind is doing the work for us as it blows air under our wings, so you and I are just along for the ride. What do you think?"

118

The young albatrix beamed. "I think this is incredible! I can't believe it! I'm flying, I'm actually flying."

And so she was, soaring alongside the big bird who was patiently drifting beside her, laboring to assist her no matter the urgency and despair he was feeling toward his own missing love.

"...farewell, Alisha Dee. If ever I have a daughter,
I hope she turns out to be just like you..."

12

"I believe you're ready," Angus declared many days
later and much farther to the north as they sat upon
the waves in the midst of a school of fine squid.

"Ready?" Alisha Dee had already eaten her fill.

"Uh-huh. Ready to go solo."

The young albatrix was stunned. "You . . . you
mean that you're leaving me?"

Angus smiled patiently. "Of course I am, child. Or
you're leaving me. You knew we couldn't stay with
each other forever, for you have your own understanding to seek. Besides, you don't need me anymore. You're a wonderful flyer, and will do very well
on your own."

"But . . . but I love you, Gus! I want to stay with you!"

"And I'd like to stay with you, too," Angus replied, remembering again why farewells were to be avoided. "But the laws of our kind, given by the Creator, cannot be ignored," he continued. "For each of us to find our own understanding beyond the far and distant horizon, we must part and make our own way. You know that."

"We . . . we could take each other for mates," the albatrix whispered shyly.

"There is little I would like better," Angus responded tenderly. "But you see, Alisha Dee, I have already given my heart to another—forever. And somewhere she is waiting for me, counting on me. It is for her that I must continue my lonely search."

120

Alisha Dee sniffed back sudden tears. "I . . . I hope you find her. But I'll m . . . miss you!"

Angus smiled with the warmth that filled his wide breast. "And I'll miss you, Alisha Dee! But I'm not dying, you know. I'm only going my own way. Remember, for us albatri this is a very small world. We'll see each other again, probably many times. And believe me, I'll be looking forward to every reunion!

"Are you . . . sure?"

"Of course I am. Now, in terms of direction, my suggestion is to keep moving westward on the trade winds until you feel the need to drop southward and catch the Westerlies. When you do, you'll discover that winter will have ended and it will be spring.

"Remember: keep your eyes on the horizon instead

of on the garbage that is always beneath you, and fly high and higher and far and farther as you seek understanding. And while you're about it, keep in close touch with the Creator, and do exactly what He puts into your heart."

Alisha Dee smiled. "Mom used to say those very words."

"It's good advice," Angus declared softly. "I would say that your mother is an uncommonly wise bird. Be proud of her, and do your best to be like her.

"Now, farewell, Alisha Dee. If I ever have a daughter, I hope she turns out to be just like you."

Alisha Dee smiled bravely. "Thank you, Gus. I'll love you always."

With a wink of his round, round eye Angus lifted his wings and was instantly airborne. "My true name," he called as he lifted upward, suddenly feeling the need to tell her, "is Angus Austin. But some call me Angus Awkward. I suppose you can guess why." Then, with a parting smile at the tearful young albatrix, he turned across the breeze and soared high and higher toward his own far and distant horizon.

121

He knew how Alisha Dee was feeling, too. He truly did. But the laws of parting from all but mates were inviolate, and it seemed to him that the least painful way to part was to simply get it done, and that meant flying away.

Besides, it was an uncommonly fine day for flying. The sky, a deep, azure blue, was scattered with puff-balls of high-flying altocumulus cloud, high-hanging remnants of a storm that had gone before him. But today there would be no storm, and for that Angus was thankful. He loved the clearness of the sky, and was even beginning to be comfortable again with the feeling of being all alone with just himself and the Creator as he glided through the vast ocean of air that was his home.

Below him on some small islands tens of thousands of cormorants were already gathering, getting ready for their spring mating rituals. From his lofty height Angus could see the great flocks of birds plainly as they left the island and dove deep into the sea after fish, leaving tiny white splashes where the water closed behind them.

With a joy in his heart that not even his loneliness for Aura Lei could diminish, Angus began speaking, as he was wont to do when flying alone, with the Creator. "O Great One," he began as he sought words to express his joy, "this is such a terrifically beautiful world you have created. The more I see of it, the more in awe I feel. It may be that I have little understanding, for I never seem able to find any. But at least I know a little of the beauty of your works.

"But not thine own, Angus Austin."

The voice in his mind was so clear that Angus nearly tumbled out of control he was so surprised. But then in an instant he realized the origin of the voice, and his heart began pounding wildly.

"O Great Creator," he breathed, "how is it that you are speaking to me?"

In Angus's mind was the sound of a divine

122

chuckle, a sound that unnerved him almost as much as had the voice only seconds before.

"As thy friend Leena Joy explained to thee, because thou art my creation," the voice declared softly. *"My Royal creation."*

"But . . . I am not Royal."

Again came the divine chuckle. *"For many days thou hast listened to thy heart concerning others. It is now time to listen to what it has to say to thee about thyself."*

"But—"

"In thy heart thou knowest that thy mate Aura Lei and all the others who have declared it unto thee were right: thou art one of a chosen generation and a Royal albatross. But the fires of thy life have not yet sufficiently burned that knowledge into understanding.

"Therefore, thou art to go down to the surface of the sea. Thine assistance there is needed badly. And perhaps, in the rendering of it, thy knowledge will be tempered with further understanding."

123

" ...Everyone is dying, and |...| can't do anything to stop it!"

13

"Gus! Am I glad to see you!"

"Lyncher X?" Angus made a tight circle above the other bird. "Will I ever stop running into you?"

"I hope not," the paddling albatross responded. "Especially when I need you so badly."

"Forget how to fly ellipses already?" Angus grinned mischievously.

"Me?" Lyncher X shook his head. "No way, Gus. But listen, we've got a real problem a few hours northeast of here."

"We?"

"Yeah, me and some others who are trying to help." Laboriously Lyncher X spread his wings and lifted into the air. "If you have time, Gus, we could really use you. So fill your gullet and follow me."

"My gullet is already full," Angus replied as he swung behind the smaller bird, hardly even thinking of the fact that his own personal detours continued to occur.

Lyncher X looked at Angus gratefully, and for some time said nothing more, simply concentrating on gaining altitude and flying as fast as he could against a fairly stiff breeze.

"It must be serious," Angus mused when at last they caught a good tailwind.

"It's awful," Lyncher X acknowledged. "Just awful! And I can't help much because I still can't fly low and slow enough. So about all I can do is bring food for the others and wait outside."

125

"Outside? Lynch, what's going on?"

"An oil slick, Gus. A tanker broke up in the storm day before yesterday, and yesterday a fishing trawler went right through the slick. You can guess the rest."

"A whole flock?"

Lyncher X nodded. "Practically all of them: gulls, petrels, shearwaters, albatri—almost everyone. I guess they were so intent on the offal that they didn't even notice the oil. Now nearly everyone's coated with it, hundreds have already died, and I don't know how much hope there is for the others. Gus, it's the worst thing I've ever seen! I can't even imagine—"

"Did you find them?"

Lyncher X shook his head. "No, I think Howie T

did. You remember Howie T? He's almost a Royal now—at least in plumage. He told me he's been puri-fying himself for about two years. Can you believe that? Anyway, by the time I got there, thirty or forty other albatri were ahead of me, most of them Royals. They're doing what they can to help, and so I put my-self on food duty for them. At least that way I can help a little."

"That's great, Lynch. I'm sure they all appreciate it."

"Oh, I don't need any thanks," Lyncher X declared, his eyes showing that the experience had truly sobered him. "You got me started thinking differ-ently, Gus, about seeking to serve instead of seeking to acquire, and . . . well, this is the right thing for me to do, and I know it! If I'm helping somebody—any-body—then that's thanks enough."

126

Angus was amazed. "You really are changing, aren't you?"

"I'm trying," Lyncher X stated, looking away. "Give me long enough, Gus, and maybe I'll become a little like you. I hope so!"

"Me?" Angus was shocked. "Hey, Lynch, you don't—"

"We've reached the slick," interrupted Lyncher X. "I hope you can help some of them, Gus. With your size and flying skills, I'm sure you can." And without further conversation Lyncher X dropped a wing and rolled into a steep dive, leaving a wondering Angus Austin to follow behind.

Moments later, as Angus flew a series of ellipses over the area Lyncher X had led him to, he was staggered by the devastation. Hundreds and hundreds of birds floated on the surface of the sea, their feathers so coated by raw crude oil that they looked like black, slimy lumps of seaweed. Most of these were already dead, for the oil had clogged their nostrils and they had suffocated quickly. The others, whose nostrils had not clogged, were still dying, but it was because the oil had clogged their feathers and pores, causing them to suffocate more slowly.

Here and there Royals were ministering to these sufferers, gliding only inches above the deadly waves as they sought to ease the last hours of the dying birds with cries of consolation and compassion.

"What can I do?" Angus asked a Royal albatrix who drifted past, her eyes filled with tears.

"What can any of us do?" she answered desolately, and Angus began then to see the hopelessness of the situation.

"Wait and watch with them, son," an older Royal declared from nearby. "They seem to take a little comfort in that."

Nodding his gratitude for the suggestion, Angus began doing slow ellipses again, this time focusing on the victims caught in the sludge who were still alive, most of whom no longer had strength even to struggle. And it was horrible. Horrible! The oil had killed indiscriminately, coating every creature who had made the mistake of diving or even just settling into the sticky morass. Most of the birds, instantly weighted down with crude and unable to get away, had struggled about in the water, getting more oil on

127

them all the time. Fortunately, death had come quickly for the majority of these. But for a few death had lingered, and as Angus looked into their hollow, staring eyes and gaping bills, his great heart felt as if it were going to break.

"My . . . egg," one Sooty gasped as Angus hung in the air above her. "My nestling is . . . is about to hatch out, and . . . and . . . there is no one."

"Your mate?" Angus asked. "Isn't he with the egg?"

"We . . . we were both following . . . the trawler. It . . . was only going to be for . . . for a few moments. He . . . he's dead! Please, find our . . . our egg."

"I'll try, ma'am," Angus responded, remembering vividly how alluring garbage had also seemed to him. "But I'll need to know where to find your nest." Angus stopped, for he could see that the bird would never tell him the location of her nest, or anything else, for that matter.

"O Great Creator," Angus wept as he watched over the newly dead mother, "why is this happening? I . . . I don't understand. And I don't understand what I can do to help. You brought me here, O Great One, but everyone is dying, and I . . . I can't do anything to stop it!"

In anguish of soul Angus moved on, from one victim to another, trying to say something—anything—that would give a small amount of comfort.

"Angus Austin?"

Looking up, Angus was not at all surprised to see

his own Royal Chosen One—the bird who had fed him and his mother so many seasons before. With a sigh of relief he lifted to the great bird's side.

"You came," the old Royal declared as though he had expected nothing less.

"As soon as I heard." Angus looked sadly about them. "But I . . . I don't see how I can help."

The great bird shook his head. "Neither do I. This is terrible, Angus Austin! In all my seasons I have never felt so helpless, so unable to render assistance. Some Royals are now trying to feed them, but alas, it is not food the sufferers want, but air for their suffocating lungs."

"Is it possible for us to move them?"

"What do you mean?"

Angus nodded at the horizon. "I was thinking that if we could somehow get some of the birds to those islands, they might be able to preen the oil from their bodies."

129

"That would be wonderful," the Royal admitted, "if only we could. Unfortunately it would do few of these birds any good, for the oil has already sealed their doom."

"But the others?"

"How would you do it, Angus? There is no way to hook them with your bill and carry them, for they are too heavy."

"But maybe if I paddled in front of them?"

The older bird sighed. "You would soon be so coated with the sludge that you could no longer paddle. And you certainly couldn't fly. No, Angus Austin, you would end up just like all these others—dead!"

"Well, somebody has to do *something!* I can't bear just watching them die!"

In frustration Angus lifted away to begin another ellipse, and it was in the first curve that he saw the male Sooty in the slick below.

"Help . . . me," the bird was gasping, and so Angus wheeled back to see what he could do.

"My mate is . . . dead," the Sooty croaked when Angus got to him, "and if I don't get back, my first-hatched chick will die too."

"Where's your nest?"

"On that island," the Sooty continued. "I . . . I can't fly, so I've been trying to paddle. Only, this oil is so thick that I can't break through it anymore."

For an instant only Angus hesitated, and then with a fierce set of his bill he settled into the sludge ahead of the exhausted Sooty. "All right," he ordered, holding his wings high to keep them out of the sludge, "I'll paddle ahead, breaking the way through the oil. You follow me!"

Without waiting for the Sooty to respond, Angus turned and began plowing through the sticky goo that seemed to have spread everywhere across the surface of the sea. His goal was the distant island the Sooty had indicated, and no matter how long it took, or what it required of him, Angus was determined to get the bird there.

It was difficult paddling, too, for the oil quickly

130

gummed about his legs and feet, causing him to expend twice the effort in going only half the distance. It was also coating the plumage on his chest and body, accumulating higher and higher toward his neck, and Angus did his best to ignore that danger and keep his wings lifted so they wouldn't be clogged.

"You following?" he called over his shoulder as he struggled forward.

"I . . . am," came the faint reply. "Thank you, Royal, for opening the way."

"Don't talk," Angus declared. "Just paddle!" And then with fierce determination he followed his own advice, for once feeling thankful for the great size his mother and the old Royal had forced upon him. Maybe now, he thought, being a huge freak would finally be worth something.

131

Frequently as he paddled he passed other oil-covered birds, but soon his exhaustion was such that Angus no longer even saw them, or noticed if they were alive or dead. He just kept paddling, until even the island that held the decimated Sooty colony seemed to become non-existant. The whole world was simply ocean, foul-smelling, oil-clogged seawater that he was doomed to paddle through forever.

Then, somehow, Angus felt like he was paddling in circles! He'd just start going straight and something would make him turn off in another direction. It was awful, but he couldn't seem to help himself. Nor could he stop the screaming and shrieking that echoed dimly in his ears whenever he did so.

But he had to keep going.

Abruptly Angus's feet struck sand and rocks, and with a sigh of terrible exhaustion and relief he threw himself onto the beach. He had made it! He had actually made it out of the slick alive.

132

... The oil on his body felt like huge stones
dragging him down...

14

"You did it, Angus Austin! You're here!"

With stupendous effort Angus opened his eyes to
see, through a red haze that was somehow misting
his vision, the big old Royal standing above him on
the shore of the island.

"Wha—"

"You did it, son. You really did it!"

"I . . . I suppose," Angus mumbled, still forcing his
legs to move. "But now we've got to get this Sooty to
his nestling."

The old Royal chuckled. "This Sooty? You'd better
look behind you, son. You've got a regular congrega-
tion in your wake."

Somehow willing his head to turn, Angus was dumbfounded to see dozens and dozens of exhausted, oil-covered birds, all making their way toward him, and then past him onto the pebbly beach. And each of them, as he or she could, mouthed a profound "Thank you" to the trembling and still uncomprehending bird.

"Where . . . where did they come from?" he gasped as he staggered further onto the beach.

"Why, you gathered them up, Angus Austin," the old Royal replied. "If you saw a bird who could still swim, you went after it. Don't you remember?"

Slowly Angus shook his head.

"Some of us were even spotting for you, Gus," a new voice chimed in. "You gathered in every bird we could lead you to."

134

Opening his eyes, Angus looked at the new bird. "Hello, Howie T," he said with a weak smile.

"Hello yourself, Gus . . . I mean, Angus Austin," Howard Theodaceous said proudly. "You did a fine thing today, something I didn't think any bird could do."

"He did something no other bird could have done!" the old Royal declared just as proudly. "No one!"

"*Help me!* Someone please help me!"

Turning at the plaintive cry, Angus saw through the haze the blurry form of a bird out in the oily waters, an oil-covered bird who was still struggling toward the shore. But the evening breeze was freshening, blowing the struggling albatross backward, away from the safety of the island.

Without even thinking Angus pushed his way back across the crowded beach and launched himself once more into the treacherous surf, his eyes seeing only the frantic bird.

"No!" the old Royal shouted fearfully from behind him, "you can't do it, Angus Austin! Let someone else."

"Listen to him," Angus's mind pleaded in agreement, "and let someone else do it."

But even as he willed himself to stop, to avoid risking his life over one other nameless bird, Angus's legs kept pumping and his huge webbed feet kept pushing the water behind. Only, he was amazed by how sluggish his body had become. Even with the wind blowing with him he had to strain to keep moving, and the oil on his body felt like huge stones dragging him down. And things would only get worse, he could see, when he got to the bird and turned into the wind. Then his condition would be critical. Still

"Angus Austin, please go back to the island and let me do this."

Bleakly Angus looked up at the old Royal who was now flying above him. "I'm . . . already covered with oil," Angus gasped. "It's better if I do it."

"Hurry," the plaintive voice called again from across the waves, "please hurry!"

"I . . . am," Angus grunted, and with more energy than he thought he had, he pushed through the last huge globs of oil and reached the besmeared bird.

"All right," he wheezed as he turned immediately back again, "follow me, and stay close!"

135

"But...but I need help."

"This is...all I can do!" Angus muttered. "If you'll stay close, I promise I'll get you to shore!"

"I...I'm not alone."

Groaning as much from frustration as from agony and exhaustion, Angus swung once more toward the terrified bird. And though he could hardly see anything at all through the red haze in his eyes, he finally made out the oil-covered form of a second bird lying low in the water, one who had apparently been dragged thus far by the other.

"Please help us," the first bird whimpered, and for the first time Angus realized she was an albatrix.

Without looking at her, and without even asking if the second bird were alive, Angus hooked one grimy wingtip with his bill and turned again toward shore. "Keep that head out of the water," he heard himself order, "and don't for a minute stop paddling. Now, let's go."

Time passed after that, an endless time of throbbing, aching muscles and giant globs of crude oil that seemed always to be directly in Angus's path. Yet somehow he rose above the pain, paying almost no attention to it. Neither did he pay attention to whether or not the albatrix was still following him. Rather he kept his bill clamped on the wing of the unconscious bird and focused his attention on the sea before him, willing his wings to stay high above the oily water while his legs and feet—now feeling like dead sticks hanging from beneath his crude-covered body—pumped their way through it.

In fact, Angus was so intently focused on clearing a pathway through the oil around him that he didn't notice the gathering flock of birds who had joined the old Royal above him, shrieking direction and encouragement.

Worse, he was still Angus Awkward, not Austin, the big, ungainly albatross who couldn't quite do anything right. And as always, the problem was with his feet. He wasn't stumbling now, but neither was he making any headway against the water and the crude. No matter how he pumped, no matter how hard he paddled, he wasn't going forward. He couldn't be, for if he were, he'd have been at the island long ago.

But continue to paddle he would, for there was no other way to save the two albatri. If it took forever he would force himself to keep paddling!

137

Paddle! Paddle!

With his eyes squeezed tightly against his pain and exhaustion, and with his great chest heaving with the need for more air, Angus willed his awkward legs to paddle.

Paddle!

Only, it was no use! His lungs were bursting, the muscles in his wings were so filled with pain from being held in their unnatural position that he could not stand it any longer, he had lost all feeling in his legs, and he didn't know how long his mind would hold out.

"O Great Creator," he gasped, "I don't mind dying, but please allow me to get these two birds to the island before I do. It's there on the horizon. I could see it if I could only open my eyes. But if you'll just give me the strength to reach beyond myself—"

And suddenly, to Angus's amazement, not his natural eyes but the eyes of his understanding were opened, and he comprehended the Creator's great commandment.

"Omasquawk," his mind gasped, his pain for the moment forgotten, "the commandment to fly far and farther isn't about height or distance, nor is seeking understanding something I must accomplish in a faraway place. It's about reaching beyond myself, stretching to do or accomplish something, or to become someone, I have never done or been before. And seeking understanding beyond the far and distant horizon is merely seeking to keep my eyes directed outward, away from myself. It doesn't mean I have to go anywhere.

"O Great Creator," he breathed, "am I right? Is it that by thinking of others, seeing to their needs instead of my own, I will find understanding?"

"*Angus Austin,*" the voice of the Creator declared softly, kindly, filling his mind and heart with love, "*thou hast found it already.*"

"I . . . I have?" Angus asked, surprised at the suddenness of the response.

"*Of course.*"

Willing his exhausted legs to continue their churning against the sticky oil, Angus pondered the words of the Great Creator. He had found understanding then? He had found it by serving others? But what

138

sort of understanding was it? And why him?

"Because thou hast lifted thyself until thou hast become Royal."

"But . . . but I don't feel Royal. I never have!"

"It always takes time," the Creator responded quietly, *"for becoming Royal is a process, not an event. Yet I now command thee to think of thyself as Royal, for by thy service to others thou hast become a Chosen One."*

"A Chosen One?" Angus blinked with surprise. "I don't understand. I *chose* to do those things, not you."

"As thou sayest."

"And that makes me a Chosen One?"

"The Creator chooseth no one until he first chooses himself," the voice declared softly. *"And choosing thyself is the beginning of obtaining divine Royalty."*

"I . . . I still don't understand," Angus's mind cried as his exhausted body lunged on.

"But thou dost understand, Angus Austin. Behold, the hearts of most of my creations are set so much upon the garbage of this world, and aspire to the pleasures thereof, that they never even think to choose themselves. But thou, Angus Austin, has set those pleasures aside, and by thine endless acts of goodness thou hast chosen thyself. And with each painful effort thou hast made in behalf of these others, for each effort requireth greater and greater love, thou hast become more and more Royal. True Royalty, as thou now seest, is pure love."

Angus was astonished. Never had he thought such a thing! Never in his wildest flights of fantasy had he imagined any of this.

139

"And because thou hast desired and chosen purity over pollution; yea, because thou hast learned not to seek thine own life but my will only, so wilt thou continue for the remainder of thy days," the Creator continued lovingly, *"each new day an opportunity to give more love, and thus to become more Royal. For the promise is now unto thee, Angus Austin, that despite the weaknesses of thy past, and despite mistakes thou mayest yet make, one day thou shalt rise to a fulness of Royalty, and know a fulness of joy in loving others. Knowing that, wouldst thou wish for any less an understanding than has been given thee?"*

As the Creator posed His question, Angus slammed into the thickest mass of oil he had yet encountered. Desperately he willed his burning eyes to open, to see his way around it. But they would not! Neither would his legs continue to paddle, nor his wings remain uplifted. He . . . he had failed! The oil had finally become so thick that he couldn't push it with his chest! But the two birds . . . he couldn't fail them! Somehow he had to find the strength—

"Thank . . . you," the exhausted albatrix said from behind him, giving Angus the first indication that he had once again reached the beach, and that it wasn't oil he was fighting to move aside, but land. And then, suddenly, his round, round eyes snapped open wide. The voice of the albatrix sounded like—but no, it couldn't be! She had gone the other way.

"I tried to stay in your wake the first time," the albatrix continued, "but you paddled too fast."

"Alisha Dee?" Angus's mind was reeling. "Is . . .

140

that you?"

"Hi, Gus. I . . . uh . . . I know you told me to go west and then south," Alisha Dee stammered in embarrassment, "but something made me . . . follow you."

"It did?"

"Yes. I wanted to be a Royal just like you, and I thought if I watched what you did—that's why I was following you. But then, when you were brought to this spill I followed you down, and the first bird I came to was my mother!"

Too surprised to respond, Angus finally looked at the bedraggled, oil-covered bird. The older albatrix, a Royal now that Angus looked past the crude on her body, appeared either dead or unconscious, and would surely have drowned had her daughter not been holding her head above water. And while Alisha Dee's wings were mostly free of the oil, her mother's wings were covered. To Angus the bird looked beyond hope.

141

"Was this her flock?" Angus asked tenderly as he waddled around the unconscious bird, carefully breaking away from her body as much of the gummy oil as he could.

"Oh, no! She told me before she passed out that she was the first to find this oil slick. But she flew too low, and one of the Sootys, trying to lunge from the oil, hit her and knocked her out of the air. She's almost dead, Gus, and I . . . I'm afraid!"

"I'm sorry, Alisha Dee. I'll clean off what I can. But if she has as much oil on her as it appears, I really don't know if we can pull her through."

"But she doesn't! She told me she didn't struggle after she fell in, but lay still, waiting for someone to come and help her."

Angus nodded. "Well, I'll do what I can."

"If Angus Austin can't do it, nobody can!" Howie T proclaimed from nearby.

"That's right!" another agreed. "The Royal can do it!" And suddenly, almost like in the old days, Lyncher X began a chant that was quickly picked up by the others:

> Angus Austin brought them home
> With strength of muscle, heart and bone.
> Without thought of self he gave
> A Royal gift, all these to save!

142

Embarrassed, Angus did his best to back away. And he would have managed it, had not the oil-covered, unconscious mother suddenly stirred. But she moved, Alisha Dee cried out, and Angus stood mesmerized.

"Angus . . . Angus Austin," the barely conscious mother gasped as she tried to lift her head and rouse herself to consciousness. "Did I hear the . . . name of . . . Angus Austin?"

"Mother!" Alisha Dee cried ecstatically. "You're alive!"

"An . . . gus Austin?" the albatrix gasped, ignoring her daughter.

Looking confused, Alisha Dee strained to support

her mother's head. "Gus...I mean Angus Austin...is the Chosen One who helped me when you didn't come back that last time," she tried to explain.

"Angus Austin? Are . . . you here?" The Royal mother was still ignoring her daughter as she tried her best to open her eyes. "Angus Austin, my darling, have I . . . have I found you at last?"

Stunned beyond belief, Angus could only stare at the poor, oil-covered bird.

"Mom, what are you saying?" Alisha Dee looked as startled as did Angus.

"Your father, child. Angus Austin is . . . is . . . Angus Austin, my sweet, are you truly here?"

Still silent, Angus did not dare to believe. He could not! He had a daughter? Alisha Dee was his daughter? And she and his beloved mate were both back in his life at the same moment? In his exhausted state he could not at first comprehend it. How could Alisha Dee's mother be his own long-lost Aura Lei? How?

"You're my *father*?" Alisha Dee questioned of Angus, her face showing her confusion. "But . . . you said you had no nestlings, no offspring."

"You didn't know?" the oil-smeared albatrix questioned, again interrupting her daughter. "Oh, Angus Austin, that's right! When we parted, neither of us knew that I was . . . that I was already carrying your egg."

Alisha Dee squealed with delight as she looked from her mother to the still silent and wondering Angus. "Oh, Father, no wonder I have loved you so dearly. No wonder I could not bear to be sent away

143

from you. This is wonderful! Wonderful!"

Then, turning back to her mother, Alisha Dee squealed once more. "Oh, Mom, I am so happy you and Angus Austin chose each other! He is the most wonderfully royal Royal in the whole world! I am so happy that the two of you have found each other again!"

At that joyful exclamation from her daughter, the Royal mother's eyes opened wide, clarity returned fully to her mind, and she found Angus and fixed him with her gaze. "Angus Austin," she breathed tenderly, simply. "My darling, darling Angus Austin!"

And at last Angus, because he could finally see beyond himself and the old Royal and his daughter and into the eyes of the sure-to-recover and still lovely albatrix who would remain his mate forever—because he could finally see the depth of love that lived and rejoiced for him there—at last he began to see what the Great Creator had been preparing him to see.

144

"Aura Lei!" he exclaimed huskily as his heart leaped with joy such as he had never known. "My beloved Aura Lei!"

And only then, with gratitude and love ascending gloriously in his huge and Royal heart, did Angus Austin finally understand.

Author's Note

For those who may have questions regarding the albatross characters in my story, the following information gleaned from two separate articles in the *Encyclopaedia Britannica* might prove interesting. In part they read:

> *Albatross,* name for more than a dozen large species of seabirds that collectively make up the family Diomedeidae (order Procellariiformes). Because of their tameness on land, many albatrosses are known by the common names mollymawk (from the Dutch for "stupid gull") and gooney. Albatrosses are the most spectacular gliders of all birds, able to stay aloft in windy weather for hours without ever flapping their extremely long, narrow wings. In calm weather an albatross has trouble keeping its stout body airborne and prefers to rest on the water surface. . . .
>
> Albatrosses come ashore only to breed in pairs in colonies on islands, where . . . pairs indulge in wing-stretching, bill-fencing displays accompanied by loud groans. . . . (There is) also a bowing and dancing display. . . . The single large, white egg, laid on the bare ground or in a heaped-up nest, is incubated by the parents in turn; one member of the pair usually remains on guard against usurpation by other home-hunting birds . . . and incubating the egg . . . while the other feeds at sea.
>
> The egg is incubated for a long period, up to 80 days. . . . Mated birds do not (usually) feed each other (during this time), but incubate in spells of several days each, the

bird at home fasting and losing weight while the bird at sea is feasting and fattening.

For the first week or so after hatching, the helpless, downy chick requires the warmth of the parental body for survival. During this period it is brooded and fed tenderly on an oily broth of semi-digested marine organisms pumped from the adult esophagus, which is muscularly constricted to control the flow to the infant's needs. Instinctively, the chick seeks the open, warm, fishy-smelling mouth of the parent, thrusting and groping blindly with its tiny bill in the open maw of the adult.

The growth of the young albatross is very slow, especially in the larger species; it attains flight plumage in 3 to 10 months, then spends the next 5 to 10 years at sea, learning navigation and feeding techniques and passing through several pre-adult plumages before coming to land to mate.

146

(The nestling) becomes very fat in the latter stages of the long fledgling period. . . . Before it leaves the nest, the chick is deserted by the parents, who retire to molt at sea. This begins a starvation period which may last considerably longer than a week. . . . When deserted, (the chick) is well-feathered and fatter and heavier than the adult; it needs a period of thinning and exercise before it is capable of flight. After days of fasting and wing flapping, it may become airborne one windy night, especially if hatched on a gale-swept . . . height from which it can flap and glide to the sea. Calm weather is its enemy; many island-born young tumble down to the sea, too heavy to take off again in still air. They are expert swimmers, however . . . (and stay on the sea until finally airborne).

Returning each year to the same nest site, the male and female remain faithful to it and thus to each other for life. It is believed that some albatross pairs also remain together at sea in the non-breeding season. . . .

Some of the best known albatrosses are the following:

Sooty albatross (Phoebetria, 2 species): (common,) wing spread to about 215 centimeters (7 feet), adult mottled sooty brown, nests on temperate sub-Antarctic islands in all oceans.

Royal albatross (D. epomophora): (rare,) wing spread to about 315 centimeters (10.5 feet), adult largely white with black outer wings, nests on islands near New Zealand and near the southern tip of South America.

Albatrosses live long, and may be among the few birds to die of old age. . . . Like other oceanic birds, albatrosses drink seawater. Although they normally live on squid, (the smaller species especially) are frequently attracted to ship's garbage. . . .[1]

147

One can see, from reading the above information, how the idea for the preceding story began to form in my mind. But because the intriguing main character who presented himself to my thinking was, of course, an albatross, as were all the associated cast of sub-characters, I quickly realized that I would need to slightly adapt the English language in order to communicate with them. The reader will have encountered two terms which survived that initial adaptation, terms I coined that so far as I know exist nowhere else, and have no meaning other than what I gave them. They are:

Albatri: plural of albatross, as in "duckbill platypi."[2]

Albatrix: a female albatross, as in, "aviatrix, a woman aviator."[3]

That being duly noted, may the Creator bless and give you your own understanding as soon as you desire it!

Blaine M. Yorgason

148

1. Encyclopaedia Britannica Micropaedia, Chicago, The University of Chicago, 1981, Vol. 1, pp. 193-194. See also: Encyclopaedia Britannica, Chicago, The University of Chicago, 1981, Vol. 15, pp. 14-19. For literary purposes, various segments of these two articles have been integrated by the author of this book into the one author's note presented here.

2. Guralnik, David B., editor in chief, Webster's New World Dictionary of the American Language, Second College Edition; Cleveland, Ohio, William Collins Publishers, Inc., 1980, p. 1091.

3. Ibid., p. 97.

"Precious moments in precious lives."®